DATE DUE

1997

The Murderer

Also by Georges Simenon
In Thorndike Large Print

Maigret and the Gangsters

The Murderer

Georges Simenon

Translated from the French by
Geoffrey Sainsbury

Thorndike Press • Thorndike, Maine

Library of Congress Cataloging in Publication Data:

Simenon, Georges, 1903-
   The murderer.

   Translation of: L'assassin.
   1. Large type books. I. Title.
   [PQ2637.I53A8513 1987]   843'.912   87-9988
   ISBN 0-89621-816-3 (lg. print : alk. paper)

Large Print edition published in North America by arrangement
with Harcourt Brace Jovanovich, Inc.

Cover design by James B. Murray.

The Murderer

ONE

So intimately blended was the sense of danger with the consciousness of everyday reality and all that was conventional and commonplace, that to Kuperus it was all the more exhilarating. It felt, indeed, very much like the effects of a strong dose of caffeine.

Dr. Hans Kuperus, of Sneek, in the province of Friesland, was once again in Amsterdam. He was there on the first Tuesday of every month. This time it was January, and he was accordingly wearing his winter coat, with a sealskin collar, and galoshes to keep out the snow.

Those details were in themselves of no importance, but they serve to show that this particular Tuesday was — so far, at any rate — just like any of the others. And when he came out of the fine red-brick station, he went straight into a bar across the way and had a glass of gin. He always did so, though he never mentioned it to anybody, since it wasn't quite becoming for a man of his position to go into a bar at ten o'clock in the morning.

It had snowed all night, and was snowing still, but the atmosphere was bright and cheerful. The flakes were far apart and floated down gently, and now and again a ray of sunshine burst through the clouds. It was freezing hard, so the snow was dry, and men were at work sweeping it up into heaps. On the canals, the water near the banks was rapidly being covered by a thin film of ice and the barges glittered with frost crystals.

The adventure began with the second glass of Bols, for that was one more than usual. He put some bitters in it to cover up the taste, because he didn't really like gin. Then he paid, wiped his mouth, turned up his coat collar, and walked out with his hands in his pockets and his briefcase tucked under his arm.

In the ordinary course of events, he should then have taken the streetcar and gone to his sister-in-law's, which was in the fashionable residential district near the Botanical Gardens. He should have had lunch there and then gone to his meeting at two.

The medical section of the Biological Association met on the first Tuesday of each month in a new building of glazed bricks that was only two streets from where she lived.

But he did not go to his sister-in-law's, the fat Madame Kramm's, nor to the meeting of the association, and this departure from the normal order of things made him extraordinarily light-hearted, as though the bonds that held him down to earth had suddenly snapped.

Strolling along the big street that led to the theater district, he stopped to look in the window of every gunsmith's. He might just as well have gone into the first one, but he went on until he must have inspected four or five, and, as he looked at the guns and revolvers, he also looked at his own reflection in the plate glass.

He looked provincial and he knew it. Particularly when he took off his hat, because he had never been able to do anything with his hair, which was fair, inclining to ginger. He was tall and broad-shouldered.

At first sight people were apt to say of him: "What a giant!"

But he knew. He had really studied himself. And in his eyes there seemed to be something soft about him. His face, for instance. Those eyelids were too heavy, those eyes too protruding. . . . And the curve of the mouth, the slightly crooked nose. . .

He was easily tired. It was caused by a deficiency. That was a word he often used, and it always impressed his patients. Phosphate deficiency was his particular form. Moreover, he knew that after walking for some time he'd have a feeling of discomfort in the chest.

That, however, was no longer of the slightest importance! With a spring in his step, he walked on to the next gunsmith's, then to another, and this time, after a cursory glance at the window, he went inside. It was quite a small shop, and a funny old man in a skullcap stood behind the counter.

"Have you got any revolvers?"

A stupid question to ask, since the window was full of them!

He handled the weapon respectfully, with a little shiver down his spine, as his patients might touch with awe the bright steel instrument he was going to use on them.

He had it loaded for him, then put it in his pocket. Looking up at the clock, he reflected that *normally* he ought at that moment to be eating cheese sandwiches and drinking tea with his sister-in-law, Mme Kramm.

The idea of going there didn't attract him in the least, and, since his train wasn't till three, he went into a good restaurant, the sort of place he would never have dreamed of entering ordinarily, considering it much too expensive. At a little table by himself, he ordered a full proper French meal, beginning with hors d'oeuvres and finishing with a *bombe glacée* and fruit. He had wine, too, which brought a flush to his face. Anyway, it was too hot in the room. He looked at his overcoat, hanging up, and thought the revolver made the pocket bulge.

He sneered.

Finally, he went into a movie house and saw the beginning of a film whose end he was never to know.

From three o'clock onward, the adventure was still more intimately blended with habitual actions, for from that time Kuperus did exactly what he would normally have done the next day. An advance of twenty-four hours — that was the only difference.

As a rule, he arrived on a Tuesday, went to his meeting in the afternoon, spent the evening at his sister-in-law's, and stayed the night there. The next morning he would do a little shopping — there were always a few things his wife had asked him to get — and at three o'clock would take the train for Enkhuizen.

A mere shift of twenty-four hours! Yet that was enough to change everything. No doubt Tuesday was market day at Enkhuizen, since the train was crowded. A different kind of people altogether from those he was accustomed to on Wednesdays. Some of them even wore

11

fur caps. Admittedly he wore one himself at Sneek, but he would never have dreamed of going to Amsterdam in one.

These strangers nodded to him, not because they knew him, but just because it's the thing to do on entering a train compartment. After that they plunged into a discussion of Danish and Latvian pigs, taking no further notice of him.

It all seemed very strange. If it had been a Wednesday, he would have had as companions in his first-class compartment the mayors of Staveren, Leeuwarden, and Sneek, who would have been to Amsterdam for the monthly conference of mayors.

Two hours by train to Enkhuizen. Several times he felt in his pocket for the revolver, and each time he could hardly repress a smile.

After that the difference between Tuesday and Wednesday was still more striking. Not that the ship was different. The same one as usual, the *Princess Helena,* was waiting alongside the quay. A fine white ship that had been in service only for the last year. Kuperus knew the captain and the other officers. The stewards, too. But today all the passengers were strangers to him.

With his briefcase still under his arm, he went below to the big saloon. It was there, at a table at the far end, that he ought now to be sitting down with the three mayors. And the steward would immediately have produced two packs of cards and then four large glasses of Amster beer.

For there was no time to be lost. It took only an hour and a half to cross the Zuider Zee. Still, they could generally count on finishing a rubber unless the mayor of Leeuwarden consistently overbid his hand, as he was apt to, particularly when he had a run of bad luck.

But this was Tuesday, and the steward merely brought him his glass of beer, at the same time remarking:

"You're a day early, aren't you?"

And it gave Hans Kuperus a peculiar satisfaction to answer:

"I'm a whole year late!"

As in the train, the people on board looked quite different from those he was accustomed to on Wednesdays. Where were they all going? Kuperus decided there must be a market day at Leeuwarden.

Darkness had fallen. The Zuider Zee was as calm as a millpond. The propeller throbbed evenly. In the saloon an Englishman was reading one of those bulky English newspapers.

A whole year late! Kuperus leaned back in his chair, reveling in the thought.

A year ago almost to the day — it was a Friday and so cold that the schools had been closed — he had received the following letter:

Esteemed Doctor,
   It is painful to see a man like you made a fool of behind his back. Someone who has great regard for you begs to inform you that every time you go to Amsterdam Mme Kuperus deceives you with one of your friends, Herr de Schutter. She goes to see him in his cottage by the canal and sometimes she even spends the night there.

The letter was badly written, but that may have been on purpose. It was by someone who knew him, certainly. But someone who didn't know him well, or he wouldn't have spoken of Schutter as his friend.

In the eyes of the world, no doubt he was. But there was no real friendship between them. Herr de Schutter was a lawyer who didn't bother to practice, since he had plenty of money without having to work for it. Like Kuperus, he belonged to the Billiard Club. In fact, he was its president, while Kuperus was only a member of the committee.

Schutter belonged to an aristocratic family. He was actually a count, though he didn't use

14

the title and even pretended to be annoyed when people addressed him by it – which, after all, was only another way of showing off.

He was the same age as Kuperus, forty-five, but he looked a good deal younger, in spite of his graying hair, because he was slim and had his clothes made by an English tailor in Amsterdam.

Schutter could speak French, English, and German, and you only had to see the photographs that hung on his walls to know that he'd traveled all over the world.

And his house! Easily the finest in Sneek. Next door to the Town Hall, which was a historic building. And Schutter's was of the same period and almost as big. It was built of black brick, and the lattice windows had pink panes, and the chimneys were made of real delft!

Schutter was on the town council. He could have been deputy mayor if he'd liked. At every election he allowed his name to be put forward, just for the pleasure of declining the honor.

Schutter had a yacht on the lake. Not a six-meter boat, or a nine-meter. Not even a *tialke*. But a big seagoing yacht called the *Southern Cross*, which had been disqualified from the regattas after having won all the races two years running.

Schutter had thin lips, which gave him a

superior smile, an indulgent smile, but one that kept you at a distance, a Voltairean smile, as some of the members of the Billiard Club used to say.

Schutter went every year to the Côte d'Azur and to the mountains. . . .

Schutter . . .

More than anything else, Schutter was the one man in Sneek who could get by with a scandalous reputation. And what a reputation! A man of whom it could be said:

"He does whatever he likes with them. . . ."

With all the women, even the married ones. Anyone else would have been cold-shouldered, blacklisted in the clubs.

But not Schutter. He was the spoiled boy of Sneek and could get away with anything.

And without even offering himself, he had been unanimously elected president of the Billiard Club, though everybody knew that Kuperus had been hankering after that honor for years.

That was Herr de Schutter in a nutshell!

And Mme Kuperus, Alice Kuperus, was a woman of thirty-five, perhaps a little stout, but pink and soft, with light blue eyes and a winning smile, commonplace and good-natured.

Kuperus had never denied her anything. She got her clothes from the same dressmaker as the mayor's wife. In fact, her astrakhan coat was easily the best-looking one in town. A little more than a year ago he had completely refurnished the living room because she had complained that it was old-fashioned, and he had even gone to the expense of a movable cocktail bar.

The ship purred on the Zuider Zee. Occasionally a bump could be heard as the bow struck a block of ice, and a scraping noise as it slithered down the ship's side.

The steward, who knew Kuperus, was waiting for the order to refill his glass.

"A cognac, please!"

That alone was almost enough to create a scandal. Never on a Wednesday had he thought of drinking brandy as he played bridge with the three mayors. But this was Tuesday! And he smiled sublimely as he thought of the revolver.

Alice Kuperus had been...

At first he hadn't believed it. And two months had gone by before he'd found out for certain. It wasn't so easy. He had to find an excuse for not attending the meeting in Amsterdam, and that was only one of many complications.

He had to pretend to catch the train. Then he had to hang around somewhere till nightfall.

17

And the trouble was that everybody knew him by sight. Then he had to hang around all the next day, because he wasn't expected home till evening. . . .

All the same, he'd done it. It was during the thaw, and he'd gone to spend the night at Hindeloopen, where his former nurse lived. She was an old woman who still wore the Friesland costume. He had thought up some kind of explanation for his visit, but she had certainly not been taken in by it.

Anyhow, he'd found out what he wanted to know. And it was true. He had seen them together, Alice and Schutter, going into his cottage by the canal, not far from the *Southern Cross*, where in the winter the lawyer gave parties.

It was a wooden building. Around it, nothing but an overgrown disused towpath and a great stretch of water, the water of the canal and then that of the first of the lakes, which in turn led to other lakes.

And it was not even two kilometers from town!

"You have no baggage?"

Kuperus almost burst out laughing in the steward's face. He would have liked to answer:

"Yes! Just one item of baggage, important, terrible, and that's in my overcoat pocket."

Through the scuttles the red and green lights of Staveren were already visible.

Two months to find out, and then another ten to decide! And perhaps he would never have decided if, two weeks before, Schutter had not been re-elected president of the Billiard Club.

Kuperus had put his own name forward. And it had been brushed aside on a show of hands. Not even a secret ballot!

For ten months he had been trying to get up his nerve to act.

He'd succeeded at last, and to prove it he was crossing the Zuider Zee in the *Princess Helena* on a Tuesday instead of a Wednesday.

"Here you are, Peter!"

He was on the point of giving the steward ten guilders, but he thought better of it. It might make him talk. Instead, he gave him one.

The journey from Staveren to Sneek was a matter of even more clockwork regularity. There were two first-class compartments, one of which he always had to himself. The three mayors stayed behind, because the mayor of Staveren entertained his two colleagues at dinner.

Getting off the boat, Kuperus went straight to *his* compartment, a smoking compartment,

19

since he smoked a pipe.

"Good evening, Dr. Kuperus."

The ticket collector must have mistaken the day, thinking it a Wednesday, since he made no comment.

The train trundled on, stopping at every station, and Kuperus had only to sit back and listen to their names being called out:

"Hindeloopen!"

Then:

"Workum!"

Which the man pronounced "Wooorekum."

Finally he would hear:

"Sneek!"

And he would find himself in the quiet little station, so clean and inviting. From there he generally went to the Groote Markt, where all would be in darkness except for the windows of the café Onder den Linden.

That was the headquarters of the Billiard Club, and he would drop in, not for a game, but to have a final glass of beer and spend a few minutes hobnobbing with his fellow members, who would invariably ask:

"Well? What's the news from Amsterdam?"

That was the normal end of the trip. This time a trifling hitch occurred, which sufficed to change everything. They had duly passed Hindeloopen and Workum. They had duly passed IJlst and were within a few minutes of Sneek when the train slowed down and then stopped altogether.

There was so much frost on the window that Kuperus couldn't see out. Opening the door, he saw a stretch of canal that he immediately recognized. They were barely five hundred yards from Schutter's cottage.

He didn't hesitate. He snatched up his brief-case, a mechanical gesture, and climbed out of the train, shutting the door behind him. Then he scrambled down the embankment. At the bottom of it, he turned and watched the train once more start up and steam off toward the town.

Dr. Kuperus had decided to make an end of it. It was practically over now, over for all three of them, for Schutter – whose Christian name was Cornelius – for Alice, and for Hans Kuperus himself.

And the instrument of this decision was in his pocket, a cold revolver, icy cold. It was not an empty idea. He'd been turning it over in his mind the best part of a year, and now he really meant business.

All around him was a blanket of snow, except for the dark patches of the canals, which were mostly unused. Some way off a tiny light, a

21

solitary light, coming from Schutter's cottage.

So he was there! Everything was moving smoothly and rapidly to the fatal conclusion.

The train had gathered speed, belching sparks into the night. Kuperus walked toward the cottage, treading cautiously as he approached. The snow was much thicker here than in Amsterdam.

So cold was it that he suddenly wondered whether his finger might not be too numb to press the trigger.

In the distance was a glow of light hanging over the town.

It was Schutter's boast that no woman could resist him, and Alice was no different from the others. She, too, came to the cottage.

And there wasn't any doubt about what she came for! Counting on the isolation of the place, they didn't even bother to close the shutters.

Looking in through the window, Kuperus saw his wife, in her underwear, drinking something, while Schutter was tying his tie.

It was a nice room. Not a bedroom; more like a studio. On the walls were photographs of Schutter in every country of the world, Schutter dressed for winter sports, Schutter as a yachtsman. On the table was a bottle of liqueur and some glasses.

Alice went on dressing in a leisurely way, as though she'd dressed and undressed in that cottage for years. At the same time, she talked, but Kuperus couldn't hear a sound through the window. He merely saw the two figures moving about, the man now lighting a cigarette, one of those cigarettes he ordered specially from Egypt, but which were no better than what anyone could buy in Holland.

Kuperus wished he didn't have his briefcase. It was in his way. On the other hand, nothing would have induced him to throw it aside. It was going to be of no further use to him, but in a confused way he felt he must not let go of anything. The briefcase was somehow part of him, and he must keep himself intact.

What would they be talking about? They chatted casually, like old lovers. After a moment, however, the conversation seemed to get more animated. It looked as though Alice was reproaching him. Perhaps he had given her grounds for jealousy. Certainly there was a sour look on her face, while on his was a stupid, conceited smile.

He stuck his pearl tiepin into his tie. He was never seen without that tiepin, which had been given to him by a maharaja. At least that's what he told them at the Billiard Club.

The moment was approaching. Alice would

23

be going. A minute or two later the front door opened. Kuperus was cold. He had taken the glove off his right hand and that hand was absolutely freezing.

Sudden darkness. Schutter had switched off the lights inside. Carefully he locked the door behind him, like any prudent householder, while Alice stood waiting.

Was this the moment?

The doctor had his finger on the trigger, but he didn't shoot.

The couple went toward the towpath that hadn't been used as such for years, since the canal was silted up and choked with rushes.

Arm in arm they walked along, and Kuperus followed. The sky had cleared a bit, and the moon shone intermittently.

He was within easy range, but still he didn't shoot. Had he perhaps thought it over for too long, worked it out too carefully?

He had pictured himself bursting into the cottage, and even making a speech...

Alice and Schutter walked in front of him, no more than ten yards away....It was she who brought matters to a head. She suddenly stopped and looked around anxiously. Schutter stopped, too.

Then at last Kuperus fired....Once...

Twice...A third time, because Schutter had only fallen to one knee. He fired the remaining three rounds to put him out of his suffering.

His heart was beating wildly. And there it was, that discomfort in the chest he always feared, an intense discomfort, which gripped him like a vise. For two or three minutes he stood absolutely still, with his left hand to his heart.

To shoot himself, he would have to reload his revolver.

One thought predominated: Schutter was dead.

Then another thought wormed its way into that one: If Schutter was dead, was it really necessary for *him* to disappear, too?

Kuperus took several deep breaths. Then he threw his revolver into the canal. He had no sooner done so than he regretted it. It was much too near the spot.

Never mind! It was done now!

He looked at his watch. There was still time to stop in at the Billiard Club.

All he had to do was push the two bodies into the water. Alice was no longer breathing. She seemed to have shut her eyes, unless it was some curious effect of the moonlight.

He set to work, anxious to get it over as soon as possible. When he thought of the Billiard

Club, his lips curled into a contemptuous smile. . . . Before pushing Schutter in, he took his wallet.

He was intoxicated, not only with what he had drunk, but still more with what he had done. His intoxication, however, instead of making him lose his head, made him extraordinarily self-possessed.

For instance, as he walked along, he considered the disposal of the wallet. After careful thought, he threw it into another canal, even older and more overgrown than the first, and he didn't forget to weight it with a stone.

One idea obsessed him: to join the four or five billiard players who would be at the Onder den Linden. He'd have a drink there. He was thirsty, fearfully thirsty, and the idea of a tall glass of foaming beer . . .

It didn't take him long to get through the outskirts of the little town. He made no plans for the future, not even for the following day.

He remembered his train ticket. Would they notice at the station that he hadn't handed it in? Hardly. But it mustn't be found on him.

In the street there was no suitable place to throw it away. After a moment's hesitation, he put it into his mouth, chewed it up, and swallowed it.

Yes, he was completely intoxicated. He could

have rolled on the ground. He could have shouted for joy. Or he could equally well have burst into tears.

What sobered him was the sight of the Town Hall and Schutter's house next to it. On the far side of the square were the lights of the Onder den Linden.

Once again he looked at his watch. He was barely more than twenty minutes later than if he'd come straight from the station in the ordinary way.

He stood under a lamppost and examined his hands. They were quite clean, thanks to the snow.

He went in. He knew in advance the glow of warmth and comfort that would welcome him there. And the waiter, Old Willem, who had been there for thirty years and who would greet him with a cheerful:

"Good evening, Doctor!"

"Good evening, Willem. Any billiard players here tonight?"

It was a well-established convention. He could hear the clack of the billiard balls, but that made no difference. He would still have to ask:

"Any billiard players here tonight?"

And Old Willem had to ask:

"Have a nice trip to Amsterdam?"

To which the proper answer, consecrated

by long usage, was:

"Glad to be back again."

And it all went off just as usual. Every bit of the ritual was performed, even to the doctor's going into the room on tiptoe because somebody was just taking aim.

Discreet handshakes in silence with the other players. The player made his shot, and tongues were unloosed.

"How's Amsterdam?"

"Same as ever. Precious little ice on the canals there . . ."

He noticed the two referees standing near the table.

"Oh, this is a match, is it?"

"Yes."

"I think I'll enter next year."

They had a club tournament every year, but Dr. Kuperus had never entered. He'd never liked the idea of playing in matches, but now, all at once . . . And for want of anything else to say, he added:

"I'm going to have another shot at being president, and I'll make a real campaign of it this time."

It was no doubt the photograph that had put the idea into his head. It hung in front of him on one of the fumed-oak pillars of the café, a photograph of all the members, with Schutter's name in red and everybody else's in black.

It was comfortable there, and he sat down in one of the luxurious armchairs.

Old Willem brought him a tall glass of foaming beer, exactly what he'd been longing for a few minutes earlier. He drank it down all at once.

"Bring me another..."

Then, turning to his neighbor:

"Anything been happening?"

"Nothing."

He had put his briefcase down on one of the tables. As a rule he stayed there about a quarter of an hour and then went home. He lived just around the corner, near the old canal.

They could hear a muffled sound of music from the movie house next door. There had even been complaints about it, because some of the players said it put them off their stroke.

Suddenly Kuperus laughed to himself. It had just occurred to him that not one of the five people in the room, or Old Willem either, had noticed that it was a Tuesday instead of a Wednesday.

Just a matter of suggestion. He always came back from Amsterdam on a Wednesday, so a Wednesday it must be!

He drank his second glass of beer, then ordered a gin.

"I've got a touch of neuralgia," he explained.

It was strange to think he would shortly be going home and his wife wouldn't be there. It would be Neel, the maid, who would open the door to him.

In her nightgown. She always went to bed early on the nights he spent in Amsterdam. He had already seen her in her nightgown. But he had never so much as made a pass at her on account of all the complications that might ensue.

Now, however?

They might come to arrest him tomorrow or the next day. In any case, it would be one day or another. So what did it matter now?

We may as well start tonight, he decided.

And with such vehemence did he make the decision that he feared he'd spoken the words out loud.

"Kuperus!"

He was being called upon to give his opinion on a shot that was the subject of dispute, the referees disagreeing. Under the tables were buckets of hot cinders to prevent the wood from warping.

"Kees swears the balls touched. . . ."

Kuperus hadn't seen the shot, but that didn't stop him from giving his opinion. Particularly since Kees was a friend of Schutter's!

"No, no! . . . Kees is mistaken. . . ."

30

And with the doctor's backing, the point was decided against the unhappy Kees, who thereby lost the match. He was crestfallen.

Hans Kuperus was just the opposite. This decision against Schutter's friend was a first taste of victory!

"Good night!...My wife must be wondering what's become of me," he managed to say.

And they'd all been so thoroughly taken in that they'd probably go on thinking it was a Wednesday and that his wife really was waiting for him.

As he went home, Dr. Kuperus thought of Neel, who was going to open the door to him in her nightgown, with her coat thrown hastily over her shoulders.

TWO

Waking up on board ship had always had a peculiar significance for Kuperus, as it had, for instance, when he had been on a cruise to Spitzbergen. To open one's eyes and realize that one was out at sea, many miles from land — there was something fascinating about that.

Something of the same sort took hold of him now. It must have been after seven, because it was already getting light and there were scraping sounds from the street, where the unemployed were clearing away the snow. Kuperus didn't open his eyes wide, only just enough to be aware of the twilight in the room.

It was his bedroom, and someone was breathing close to him. Someone was sleeping at his side, and it wasn't Alice Kuperus, but Neel, the servant, and it was Neel's warm leg that touched his own.

What had happened to the world? Henceforward, every day, every night, Kuperus could share his bed with Neel, or with anyone else, for that matter.

He wondered what effect it would have on her. Would she take advantage of it to lie in bed all morning? Or would she go about her work as usual?

Her breathing changed. She sighed, stretched an arm, then snuggled down under the bed-clothes again. A moment later, however, she thrust one leg out of the bed, then the other.

Her movements were no doubt just the same as on other mornings, when she woke up in her attic. For half a minute she sat on the edge of the bed, only half awake, her eyes dull, her limbs heavy. She turned around to look at Kuperus, who pretended to be asleep, then started putting on her stockings.

She went downstairs without washing, and he heard her lighting the kitchen fire, then making the coffee.

As for Alice Kuperus, she was dead and done with! So was Schutter!

Had Neel been aware of their liaison? When he had returned home the previous evening, he had asked:

"Is my wife in bed?"

And he was surprised to hear himself act the part so convincingly.

"Madame is not here," Neel had answered.

"What? Where is she then?"

"She got a telegram from Leeuwarden to say her aunt was ill. . . ."

"When do you expect her back?"

"Madame said she'd return tomorrow."

But he knew better! She wasn't coming back tomorrow, or the next day, or the next. . . . Did Neel guess what was going to happen? She murmured:

"Can I go back to bed?"

"Make me a cup of tea first. Bring it to my room."

To think that she'd been in the house for three years, and that every time she'd passed him he'd wanted to lay hands on her but had never dared! He'd felt sure she was an innocent girl, probably ignorant.

"Don't hurry away," he said when she brought the tea. "Come over here . . . You needn't be afraid."

"I'm not!" she answered.

Indeed she wasn't! And it wasn't the first time that sort of thing had happened to her! Kuperus was nervous, not because of her, but because of everything. After all, he had plenty of reason to be. But his nervousness was translated into an amorous frenzy, which provoked Neel to remark:

"You're pretty hot stuff!"

At last the door opened and Neel came in with his breakfast on a tray. She put it down beside him, then went over and drew back the curtains, revealing the black branches of a tree against a leaden, snowy sky.

She had had time to wash and dress. Her hair was neatly done, and she had put on a clean apron. Her arms were pink and smelled of soap.

Dr. Kuperus would have been at a loss for an answer if he'd been asked whether she was pretty. She had the prominent cheekbones of a peasant, and her features were not well drawn. Certainly she was not a classic beauty, but in her sturdy, buxom way she was desirable, and his eye ran over her figure greedily.

"What time is it, Neel?"

"Eight o'clock, Doctor."

She answered exactly as she would have on any other day, and that was reassuring.

"What's the weather like?"

"It looks as though we're in for some more snow.... Which suit will you be wearing?"

"The black one... Look here, Neel..."

"Yes, Doctor?"

"Didn't it seem funny to you to be sleeping in my bed?"

"Why should it?"

"Have you had many men before?... Listen,

Neel...I'd like to know something: at what age did you start?"

"At fifteen. I was a nursemaid then, looking after some children in Amsterdam."

"And since then?"

"Since..."

She shrugged her shoulders, as though she regarded it as a matter of small importance.

He got up, shaved, and dressed. And all the time Neel ran through his thoughts. He looked at himself in the mirror more critically than usual and decided that his face was rather puffy. It was inclined to be at times, and it always worried him.

What was going to happen now? He stood staring out the window at the canal and the bare trees along its banks. Downstairs, the doorbell rang, and by the sounds that followed he knew that his first patient had been shown into the waiting room.

The most important thing was for him to go on being surprised by his wife's absence, and after a reasonable time – a day or two – to report it to the police. It wasn't going to be difficult. He could tell that from the way he'd succeeded with Neel. He felt himself playing his part to perfection. And the funny thing was that never in his life before had he been a good liar!

What was there that could give him away? Nobody had seen him. Nobody could guess that he had got out of the train between stations.

Downstairs, he went into the living room. The sight of it almost made him smile, because it had its place in the story. It was just over a year ago that Alice's complaints about her old-fashioned living-room furniture had reached their height. At first he had turned a deaf ear to them. The room was really in excellent condition, and he didn't see why he should go to such needless expense.

Then suddenly one day he had changed his mind.

"All right, you can have your new furniture."

It was exactly three days later that the anonymous letter arrived. Just when Alice was up to her ears in fabric samples, in catalogues, wallpapers, velvets...

In his office, his first act was to change into a white coat. He glanced into the waiting room, where there were already five people. Later on there would be more like twenty, since he was a popular doctor and charged only one guilder for a consultation.

He was pleased with himself. There he was, cool and dignified, just as if nothing had happened.

A woman brought in a small boy whose face was covered with scabs. The doctor had picked up his pad to write out a prescription when a sudden pang darted through his breast.

Someone knew! At least there was someone who was bound to know sooner or later. He had thought of everything except that. How could he have overlooked it?

It was the person who had written the anonymous letter. And he hadn't the faintest idea who it could be. He didn't even know whether it was a man or a woman.

Whoever it was, he or she would instantly jump to conclusions on hearing of the double murder.

Who *could* it be? One of the members of the Billiard Club? Why not Neel? Neel could hardly fail to have known.

What had been occupying his thoughts so far? It was terrible to think he could overlook a question as important as that. Certainly Neel must have been aware of what was going on, since Alice had left each time the doctor went to Amsterdam. And she'd never breathed a word.

Obviously Alice must have paid her to keep her mouth shut. . . .

He had forgotten all about the prescription. Looking up, he wondered for a second what the scabby child was doing standing there in front of him. Then, with an effort, he pulled himself together, wrote out the prescription, and opened the door to the next patient, an old man with intercostal neuralgia.

Suppose it was Neel who had written the anonymous letter...

He wasn't mistaken: he had twenty-two patients during the morning. As usual, he interrupted his work at eleven for a cup of tea and a slice of bread.

It was served in the dining room, which smelled of polish, because it was the day for doing the floors. But he had no sooner drunk the tea down than he felt impelled to go into the kitchen.

"Is there anything you want?" asked Neel.

The strange thing was that he still desired her. All he could think of saying, however, was:

"Isn't my wife back yet?"

"No, not yet...I thought she'd be back before now...."

His day's work wouldn't be over till five, when he'd be able to join his friends in the Onder den Linden. No doubt they'd talk of Schutter.

He had lunch alone, watching Neel in the mirror when she brought in the dishes.

"Did you like it last night?"

"Why do you ask me that?"

"Would you like to do it again?"

"You know very well we can't. Not when Madame comes back...If she found out..."

Suppose they did put him in prison, what would that matter? He knew the examining magistrate, Anton Groven, who was also a member of the Billiard Club. A bad player, because he was terribly near-sighted. He would be on one side of the table, and Kuperus with his lawyer on the other. Would he call him Hans, or would he have to start all at once calling him Dr. Kuperus?

In the afternoon the doctor went out to make his calls. He wore his fur coat and carried a little bag with his instruments. On the big canal there were dozens of boats moving around, fighting for berths, and making a fearful noise with their diesel engines.

It was the day of the cattle market, and they were bringing animals from all over the countryside by the many canals that converged on Sneek.

Kuperus had to pass the Town Hall, and with a new interest he looked at Schutter's house. It was the only house in the town where there were two servants: a footman in a striped waistcoat and a butler in evening dress who wore white gloves when he waited at table!

At the doctor's there was only Neel and a cleaning woman who came in twice a week.

Could it have been the cleaning woman who had written the anonymous letter? He'd really never looked at her. He merely knew her vaguely by sight as a homely old body. A bright red face and untidy hair over a bundle of voluminous black petticoats.

A case of scarlet fever, then a woman who was expecting a baby, probably next day, possibly that very night...During December he'd been called out at night exactly twenty-six times for deliveries.

When he finally got to the café at five o'clock, he was tired out. There was no particular reason why he should have been; the day's work had been no heavier than usual. Only, his life seemed to have suddenly slipped into a higher gear and to be going at an excessive speed.

He put his bag down in the corner as usual, and Old Willem helped him off with his fur coat. He shook hands with Pijpekamp, then with Van Malderen and Loos.

"It looks as though we won't get any skating this winter," said Van Malderen, the lawyer. "We no sooner get a good frost than it thaws again."

41

In the quiet billiard room was a clock that had always impressed Kuperus. It was high up on the wall. There was nothing remarkable about its face, which was marked in ordinary roman figures. But under it was a huge brass pendulum which always caught the light, and it seemed to him, as he looked at it, that in that room the seconds went more slowly than anywhere else.

And there was some truth in it. There was something about the Onder den Linden that made the time pass slowly and serenely. Even before you reached it you were already struck by the hushed dignity of the square, deserted at that time of night, brooding under the Gothic tower and gilded turrets of the Town Hall.

Old Willem walked noiselessly across the parquet floor, which was more highly polished than any other. Highly polished, too, were the little tables all around the room against the walls. Everything shone. Everything basked in an atmosphere of warmth and well-being, including the proprietor, Loos, who, when there was nobody there, would settle down snugly in one of the easy chairs beside the big square stove, put on his glasses, and read the *Telegraaf* for hours on end.

It was a place where you could sit and smoke with two or three others without bothering to keep up a conversation. Just a phrase from time to time; that was enough. And, as often as not, it was answered merely with a grunt. Some, like Van Malderen, kept their pipes there in the rack, and their jars of tobacco. But on the whole it was the smell of cigars that dominated, blended with that of gin.

"Hasn't Schutter turned up yet?"

It was Kuperus who asked the question, as he lit his pipe, staring into the fire through the mica panes. The lights were already switched on over the main billiard table, the one on which all the tournament games were played, which had very handsome carved legs.

"He hasn't been seen since yesterday," said Loos, poking the fire, at the same time puffing away at his pipe.

And in a leisurely way he went on:

"The funny thing is that his butler came around a little while ago to ask if he'd been here. . . ."

Van Malderen winked. He was the wag of the club. He had a large stock of funny stories, which he would relate with a mournful air that suited him perfectly. He was thin and colorless, and made a point of dressing like a Protestant pastor.

"Another woman . . ." he sighed. "Fortunately, I have nothing to worry about myself.

My wife is much too plain to get into trouble!"

It was quite true! And it was a great source of satisfaction to him.

"Well?" asked Kuperus. "Who'd like a game?"

"For how much?"

"One guilder..."

"All right," said Van Malderen, and both men took off their jackets and slipped elastic bands over their shirt sleeves. Each had his own personal cue, padlocked to the rack.

"Let's make it two hundred up."

In the middle of the game, two or three others came in, one of them the wholesale tobacconist from next door, who, as he shook your hand, would manage to leave a cigar in it, saying with a chuckle:

"Try that one."

Kuperus took the lead at once, starting off with a break of sixty. There was a big mirror in the room, and every time he took aim he glanced at himself.

To think that he'd killed Schutter! He didn't think half so much about Alice. Somehow that was much less serious. It only belonged to his private life.

While with Schutter...They began talking about him while Kuperus was making the winning break.

"The mayor told me Schutter's going to run

44

in the next election. . . ."

"For what party?"

"The Progressives, of course."

Schutter, just to tease them, or out of some sort of snobbery, dabbled in left-wing opinions, Schutter who had his dinner served by a butler in white gloves!

"Schutter loves an opportunity to hold forth," said Kuperus, leaning over his cue.

But what he really thought was:

Schutter *loved* an opportunity. . .

"He's a very able man. There's no doubt about that. . . . Succeeds at anything he puts his hands to. . . I bet he gets in. . . ."

"And I bet he doesn't!"

That was Kuperus again, still at the same break, still counting out loud after every stroke.

"He ought to have a good chance," said another. "The retiring member's seventy-two."

"And Schutter?"

"He's the same age as me," broke in Kuperus once more.

He simply couldn't help it. And each time he spoke, he looked at himself in the mirror.

It was wonderful. He was at the top of his form. The puffiness had gone from his features. At the corner of his mouth was the faintest hint of a smile, so slight that only he could see it.

"Forty-four?"

"No. Forty-five."

"He doesn't look it. . . . But of course he takes cares of himself."

"Even as an undergraduate," Kuperus said, "he used to polish his fingernails. . . . Two hundred . . ."

He had won the game. A moment later he was pocketing the guilder Van Malderen handed over with a humorous gesture of reluctance, saying:

"I'll have to think up an explanation, or my wife'll be getting after me about my extravagance."

He loved to say things like that, though everybody knew that Mme Van Malderen was a meek and mild creature who never dared make the least hint of reproach.

"I don't know what my wife's up to," ventured Kuperus. "I was told she got a telegram yesterday and has gone to see an aunt of hers in Leeuwarden. . . ."

"So you're enjoying yourself, I suppose!" joked Van Malderen.

Perhaps *he* was the person who'd written the anonymous letter?

It was a pity it hadn't been kept. Kuperus had torn it up into little bits and thrown them in the fire. He couldn't remember what the handwriting looked like. . . .

Yes, Van Malderen was just the sort of person to do a thing like that. He'd think it very amusing, and be quite content to keep the joke to himself. He'd never let it out, though he might very well throw out a few ambiguous remarks, like the one just now:

"So you're enjoying yourself, I suppose!"

The door opened, and the men exchanged glances. A young woman had entered and, apparently indifferent to the clouds of smoke, sat at one of the tables on the far side of the room and ordered a liqueur.

"Do you serve dinner here?" she asked.

Willem answered yes, but it obviously went against the grain to do so. For the young woman was not only a blonde, but a very artificial one, and was dressed as no woman ever dressed in Sneek. Her lips were rouged and her heels were so high that it was a mystery how she kept her balance on them.

She produced a gold cigarette case and lit a cigarette. That she came from Amsterdam was obvious. With an amused eye and without the slightest embarrassment, she looked around the café, which was in all respects designed to be a haven of refuge for the male sex and in particular for the worthies of the town.

"Waiter!"

Willem ran forward, his napkin over his arm.

"Do you know where Count de Schutter lives?"

"The... Count?" stammered Willem. "If you mean Herr Cornelius de Schutter..."

"That's the name."

Everybody listened. There was no sound but the roaring of the stove.

"He lives a hundred yards from here, Madam. Next door to the Town Hall."

"Has he got a telephone?"

"It would be quicker to go there."

"That's not what I wanted to know. I asked if he had a telephone."

"Yes... The number's 133."

"Can I phone from here?"

"To the right of the washrooms."

She got up, flicked the ash off her cigarette, and crossed the café. All eyes were on her, but that didn't seem to bother her in the least. She went into the phone booth and shut the door, after which there was a faint ring and then a confused murmur.

The men looked at each other. Van Malderen made Willem a sign to fill up the glasses.

"That's another one!" sighed Loos.

"Perhaps he expected her," suggested Van Malderen. "And that's why he's made off...."

The young woman returned and asked Willem: "Have you got any rooms?"

48

"No, Madam...This isn't a hotel. But I can call the Station Hotel....It's very comfortable. All the rooms have running water."

"Give me another cherry brandy first."

She looked anxious. Three young men came in to play billiards, but they had nothing to do with the Billiard Club. They weren't much to look at, and they made an unnecessary amount of noise to cover their self-consciousness, laughing and talking without a break.

"Waiter?"

"Yes, Madam?"

"Does Count de Schutter come here often?"

"Every day."

"Did he tell anybody he was going away?"

"No, Madam."

Loos got up. This was really a matter for the proprietor to deal with.

"He was here yesterday around three o'clock," he said. "And I was surprised not to see him today. Even more so when his butler came around to ask if we had news of him."

Kuperus was torpidly lolling in an easy chair, his feet against the stove, smoking a cigar that the wholesale tobacconist had slipped into his hand. He looked quizzically at the young woman from Amsterdam.

Somehow she didn't attract him, though he couldn't explain why. For there was no denying it: she was beautiful. It was curious. There was all the difference in the world between her and Neel, the badly dressed and almost ungainly Neel, with disheveled hair. Yet it was Neel's ample figure that made him go hot all over. He thought of her again now; there was a matter that had to be decided.

Would he dare have her sleep with him again that night? It wasn't so simple as all that! Today he was supposed to be expecting his wife at any moment. He must look as though he were expecting her, and he must show increasing anxiety when she failed to show up. Perhaps he ought to have shown some already.

"Willem!... Will you look in the book and see if Mme Costens, in Leeuwarden, has a telephone."

Mme Costens was the aunt in Leeuwarden who was supposed to be ill. It was only natural he would telephone her to ask about Alice.

He had seen her only a couple of times. She was a fat and rather vulgar woman whom Alice rarely referred to, since she kept a fish store.

Obviously a fish store would have a telephone! Willem turned over the pages of the directory. Kuperus smoked his cigar, thinking of Alice, though he still went on looking at the blonde stranger.

There was a connection between them.

Schutter! By what inexplicable aberration had the latter picked on Alice Kuperus? What had he found in her to get excited about?

And, on her side, how on earth had Alice – Alice of all people – come to plunge into an affair of that kind? The more he thought of it, the more preposterous it seemed. She was the very last sort of woman to commit such folly.

She looked like a bonbon. She was sugary to the core. She stuffed herself with pastries, and her skin was as pink as sugar icing. For a week at a stretch she could fuss and fiddle with samples before buying a new pair of curtains.

She ate a particular brand of chocolate because in each package was a picture of a flower, a common chromolithograph, which she would paste into an album.

"Is this it?" asked Willem. "Costens, fishmonger?...Shall I get it for you?"

"Please."

The young men were really too noisy. Van Malderen sighed comically as he looked at the girl from Amsterdam.

"It must be a wonderful thing to be a bachelor....I've never been one...."

"Except before your marriage."

"Not even then! I had a mother, a saintly woman whose one thought was to keep me pure for my future wife."

"Did she succeed?"

"Most of the time..."

"Madame Costens is on the phone."

"Is that you, Aunt?...I hope you're better....
What?...What's that?...Alice isn't there?"

He acted the part to the full, though for himself alone, since he could be neither seen nor heard by the others. He assumed an expression of astonishment, then of anxiety. When he returned to his friends, he was the picture of bewilderment.

"I don't know what to make of it....Willem!
Bring me a gin."

"What's the matter?"

"It's unbelievable...."

He lowered his voice, and went on:

"My wife was supposed to be in Leeuwarden.
She isn't there...."

He gulped down his glass of gin and looked at himself in the mirror.

"Who told you she was there?"

"Our maid."

"Doubtless she got mixed up," suggested Loos. "Your wife's probably gone to some other aunt's...."

"She hasn't got another."

Van Malderen's lips were pursed in a comic grimace.

"Excuse me...I'd like to be alone, to

think this over. . . ."

As he left the café, he looked really upset. The expression remained on his face until he turned the corner, when it suddenly faded away. All at once his face was completely expressionless.

What expression ought it to have? He really didn't know. It was easy in front of the others. But now? . . .

And what was he to do next? It was still too soon to go to the police. For the moment, the only thing was to go home. He'd find Neel there. . . .

He ate dinner as usual. The light over the dining-room table had a huge shade of pink silk, which made the whole room pink and cozy.

"Isn't my wife back yet?"

"No, Doctor."

"Any telephone calls?"

"Only one, asking you to go to the Meeuses' as soon as possible. Their daughter's worse. . . ."

"Neel!"

"Yes."

"Look me straight in the eye, Neel! . . . Madame never went to her aunt's in Leeuwarden. . . . You knew that, didn't you?"

"Yes, Doctor."

She answered quite simply. And she looked him straight in the eye, just as he'd asked her to.

"Where's she gone then?"

"I don't know. She didn't say."

"You've no idea?"

"No, Doctor."

"Come here."

She was in her white apron. Still munching his food, he put his arm around her waist.

"Do you love me a little bit, Neel?"

"What are you leading up to?"

"We had a good time last night, didn't we?"

"That question again!"

"You'd like some more, wouldn't you?"

"And when Madame comes back? What then?"

"Doesn't she do as much herself? Well? What's your answer to that?"

"Of course she does."

"You knew it?"

"Of course."

"And what did you think about it?"

"I thought that when a woman had all she could want..."

Her eye ran over the comfortable furniture, the silver on the table.

"Go on."

"I thought there was no point in it."

"No point in what?"

"In deceiving you."

"Sit down."

"Me?"

"Yes, you . . . Sit down and have your dinner with me."

"I'd rather not."

"Why?"

"It's not the right thing."

"You didn't mind coming to bed with me!"

"That's different. . . . Besides, I've got things to see to in the kitchen. . . . You're not angry, are you?"

Left alone, he looked at himself once again in the mirror. He was hot all over. He was afraid. It was difficult to say what he was afraid of. Not of going to prison, anyhow.

Yet he was afraid. A vague fear gripped him, rather like the discomfort that gripped him in the chest.

He gobbled his food without really enjoying it, then went and opened the kitchen door.

"Haven't you finished?"

"I've still got a few things to wash up."

"Leave them till morning. Come."

It was an absolute necessity. He couldn't bear the thought of being left alone.

"Suppose Madame turns up?"

"She won't."

He oughtn't to have said that. Never mind!

"Come on, my big girl . . ."

It was stranger than the Spitzbergen boat! They were right out at sea, far from land. The whole house, with its darkened rooms and the single lamp by the bedside, floated in a new, unknown, and incoherent universe in which a few solid facts stood out, like Neel's pink chemise as she sat on the edge of the bed taking off her stockings, her hair hanging over her face.

Where were they heading?

Neel's mouth, like Alice's, had the taste of chocolate. The same exact chocolate!

THREE

Everyone agreed that he was behaving with great dignity in his unenviable situation. So much so that no one thought of laughing at him. On his side, he was hardly conscious of having to act a part. He simply did what obviously had to be done, and did it naturally.

He duly called on the superintendent of police, a tall thin man he'd known for many years, who always wore a morning coat. Considering his errand, Kuperus had no cause to be gay, and in this he was helped by the superintendent, who was by nature gloomy.

"Sit down. How are you?"

"All right, thanks."

"And Madame Kuperus?"

"That's just it! I don't know. . . . I've come to report her disappearance. She's been gone two days. . . ."

He spoke like one who has an unpleasant duty to perform. And his air of annoyance was naturally construed as being the restrained expression of a great inward grief.

"That's strange," muttered the superintendent, looking into the fire.

"That my wife should disappear?"

"That you should report the fact just after I received a similar report concerning one of your friends, Schutter, the lawyer...."

Kuperus shrugged his shoulders, as much as to say there could be no connection between the two. He didn't even find it funny to see the superintendent swallow everything he said, look at him with compassion, and at the end give him a long insistent handshake.

"I promise I'll do everything in my power.... Meanwhile, we must hope for the best. There may be some misunderstanding...."

Kuperus thanked him with a wan smile. Outside, he stopped in front of a pharmacy, in the window of which was nothing but an immense yellow jar. Looking in, he examined himself in the glass and was surprised to discover that he looked every inch a widower.

If he hadn't gone to the Onder den Linden at five o'clock, his absence would have been readily understood, but he considered it, on the contrary, to be absolutely necessary. He put down his bag in the corner, surrendered his coat to Old Willem, and said:

"It really is freezing now."

It was. Early in the morning a hard frost had set in, and ice was rapidly forming on the canals that cut Sneek up into rectangles. Who could know that there was something providential in that frost? Nobody! And that's why Kuperus repeated to one after the other as he shook hands with them, to Van Malderen, to Loos, and to a couple of others:

"It's freezing hard."

He noticed that the blonde woman was there again, sitting in the same place, and that she looked at him with what seemed to be a hostile stare. Because it was the second time he'd seen her, he thought it was only polite to bow slightly as he caught her eye.

"Well?" asked Van Malderen in the same tone in which he might have said "My poor friend."

Kuperus answered with a sigh. He sat down and lifted his feet for Willem to take off his galoshes.

"It's in the paper," murmured Van Malderen after a silence.

"What? They speak of my wife?"

"No! About Schutter," and he read out:

"The well-known lawyer Cornelius de Schut- ter has disappeared without leaving the

slightest trace. It is still hoped however that it will turn out to be nothing more serious than an unpremeditated journey undertaken on some sudden whim. . . ."

Kuperus turned around, conscious of someone behind him. It was the blonde, standing and looking at him with a worried expression.

"You're the husband, aren't you?"

"Whose husband?"

Van Malderen turned away, because he found it difficult to keep a straight face. Only Kuperus remained perfectly natural, incredibly natural.

"The husband of the woman who's gone off with Cornelius."

He began by lighting his cigar, during which time his features became still graver and more dignified. Then he looked around him as though he were at bay.

"I am not prepared to admit anything of the sort. We are all miserable sinners, of course, but, until the matter is proved to have foundation, I cannot allow anyone to throw doubt on my wife's honor. . . ."

If the subject hadn't been so serious, there'd have been a burst of applause. But the young woman showed her impatience. She was not the elegant traveler of the previous day. In both

60

attitude and voice she was decidedly common.

"Anyhow, you have no idea where they've gone to?...A nice mess I'll be in if he doesn't turn up again!"

She looked at all the men present, as though holding them personally responsible for her plight.

"We're all very sorry, I'm sure..." murmured Kuperus.

He played billiards, which everybody thought showed great fortitude. There was no doubt he was taking it very well.

To tell the truth, he was thinking of Neel.

All the rest was of minor importance.

Kuperus spent his mornings in his office as usual and called on his patients in the afternoon. He spent an hour or two at the café with his friends, then read the *Telegraaf* while he had his dinner. The temperature was below freezing. He wasn't tempted to go back to the spot to make sure there were no traces.

His windows looked onto the canal, where he could see the bargemen breaking the ice around their barges every morning. The children wore bright-colored hats and mufflers, and rubber boots. Steps rang out with peculiar insistence on the frozen cobblestones.

A police inspector came, as serious and

respectful as the superintendent. Kuperus gave him a glass of wine, since he happened to have a bottle warming up at the side of the grate. The inspector produced a little notebook and a pencil.

What dress was Mme Kuperus wearing when she left the house?...What was her coat like, her hat?...At what time did she leave?...

"I'll call the servant," said the doctor.

It was Neel who answered the questions. She was much more upset by them than he was. Indeed, she seemed nervous that day. At dinnertime she dropped a plate and broke it, and during the meal, when he tried to draw her to him, she snapped:

"I wish you'd behave yourself."

When talking to him, she was less and less respectful. When the inspector had gone, she came into the room without having been called. She was a country girl, and the mistrustful look on her face was typical of a peasant.

"Can I speak to you for a minute?"

"What is it, Neel?"

"I ought to have told you before....I think it would be better if I didn't spend the night in your room....The other thing doesn't matter, but if I sleep in your bed it's bound to get around sooner or later....It makes me feel awkward....Well! There it is!..."

"Why do you tell me that now?"

"Because...I really don't know."

"Why didn't you say so yesterday or the day before?"

She shrugged her shoulders before answering:

"Do you really want to know?...It's all the same to me."

"All right. Out with it..."

"It's Karl who doesn't like it....You're a lot wiser now, aren't you?...Karl's my young man...."

"And it's today that you're going to see him?"

Another shrug of the shoulders.

"No."

"He knows about...about you and me?"

"Naturally."

"And that's why you don't want..."

She fidgeted impatiently.

"No, no! You've got it all wrong....I'm sure you won't turn me out of the house, so you may as well know....Karl's been sleeping in the house for the last five months."

"What do you mean? Where?"

"In my room."

"How does he come in? How does he go out?"

"I..."

She blushed, hesitated, then blurted out hurriedly:

"I had a key made for him. He comes in late

at night, when everyone's in bed, and goes off early again next morning."

"And he's been here these last few days?"

Neel nodded. He was completely taken aback. He felt thoroughly shaken, and to pull himself together he poured a glass of wine.

"Would you like some, too?"

"No, thanks. I don't like red wine."

"What sort of man is he?"

"Karl?...A German. From Emden..."

"And what does he do?"

"Nothing...Occasionally, when there's a banquet, he's taken on as an extra waiter."

"Leave me alone now, will you?"

"Am I free tonight?"

"Yes...Or, rather, I don't know....I'll tell you later...."

He sat down in the easy chair in front of the fire. The pink lampshade bathed the room in warm light. Every bit of furniture was dusted and polished. The glasses glittered on the sideboard. Brass ornaments glowed richly. On the mantelpiece was a pile of cigar boxes.

Kuperus couldn't remain seated for long. He jumped to his feet. He opened his mouth to shout something, but was stopped by the sight of himself in the mirror.

It was inconceivable! It upset everything. It was absolutely unheard of! So much so that for a moment he wondered whether Neel hadn't been romancing.

For five months a man had been sleeping in his house every night without his having the faintest suspicion. They had been thinking they had the house to themselves, and all the time...It was outrageous! And Kuperus, until the last few days, had religiously kept his hands off Neel for fear of complications!

This man, this Karl, had a key to the front door! And, more improbable, more outrageous than anything else, he was still coming, even since the change had begun, sleeping all alone on Neel's iron bedstead, while she...

He rang for her. The folding doors were open between the dining room and the living room, and as he talked he walked up and down from one room to the other.

"Does he love you, this man?"

"I think so."

"Isn't he jealous?"

"I don't know."

"Anyhow, he accepts the fact that you come to bed with me?"

"That's different."

"What's different?"

"You and Karl. After all, you're the master. He's intelligent enough to see that it's necessary."

"All right. You can go."

"And tonight?"

"Tonight you'll sleep with me. Do you hear? It's necessary, as you put it so nicely!...And now, for the love of God, clear out!"

He was at the end of his tether. Never would he have believed it would have such an effect on him. Here he was, jealous of Neel. That's what he'd come to! He was actually suffering because she had said that their relations were of no importance.

It was impossible to come to any other conclusion. And he was alarmed by it. He sensed some hidden danger. To calm himself, he went out and walked along the deserted quays by the canals.

Suppose it was this man, this Karl, who had written the anonymous letter. Some sort of criminal type, no doubt. Couldn't be far short of it – a man who did no work and had no home. How long would he wait before he started trying to blackmail him?

Dr. Kuperus passed the Onder den Linden, but merely peeped through the window without going in. Games were in progress at all four billiard tables, since they were approaching the finals of the billiard tournament. Near the bar, the blonde woman was sitting with Van Malderen and another man, who had his back to the window.

"Bring me my tea," called out Kuperus as he went upstairs to his bedroom that evening.

He had never taken tea at night, but it had served, in the first place, as a pretext for getting Neel into his room, and from then on it had become an established custom.

He changed into his dressing gown. A little later Neel came up with a tray, which she put down on the table without looking at him. Then, with a scowl on her face, she started undressing.

"Is he upstairs?"

"Yes."

"What did he say?"

"Nothing. What did you expect him to say?"

She pulled back the covers and got in bed, lying on her back with her hands under her head.

"What does it matter to you what I do *afterward*? What difference does it make whether I sleep here or there?"

He went on brushing his teeth without answering.

"You're not jealous, I hope."

He started and shot a glance at her as she lay there looking sulkily at the ceiling.

"And what about you? Do you love him?"

"I don't know."

"What's he like?"

"Tall and very thin, with bright eyes."

"You don't know what he was doing in Germany?"

"No. But he told me he'd got into some sort of trouble. He's not just anybody. He's educated."

"Where did you come across him?"

"In the street...He followed me when I was out doing the shopping."

"How long ago was that?"

"Five months."

If it was true, he could not have written the anonymous letter. Kuperus got into bed. He was conscious of the warmth of her body, which was nonetheless apathetic.

"Neel!"

"Yes."

"Answer me honestly...Are you the same with him as with me?"

"In what way?"

"Frigid...As if you don't feel a thing...."

"Yes."

It was true. She had answered without a moment's hesitation, and her voice had sounded sincere. Besides, she wouldn't have taken the trouble to lie.

"What would have happened if we'd discovered this Karl when my wife was here?"

"I'd have been kicked out."

"And suppose you hadn't been able to find another place?"

She sighed. It was her way of saying that she really didn't care and that all these questions were a bore. She wasn't in a good temper at all, and she stared at the ceiling more obstinately than ever.

"What does he do all day?"

"How should I know?"

"I suppose it's you who keeps him in food?"

"Of course! There's always enough left over."

He preferred not to think of that, because it reminded him of the mystery that had for a considerable time been a worry to Alice, that very question: What happened to all the food left over? It was explained now. But it was too late.

"What do you think of me, Neel?"

"Why should I think anything in particular?"

"Tell me the truth. I mean it. Really."

"I know. . . . It's funny."

"What's funny?"

"Let's go to sleep."

"I asked you what was funny."

"You! All you do. The way you behave with me. . . Everything, in fact. I really can't explain it. . . . Are we going to do anything or are we going to sleep? . . . I've got to be up by seven o'clock in the morning."

He'd have liked to be able to answer:

"All right! If that's how you feel, you can go to sleep."

But he couldn't. She had found the right word for it. It was necessary.

For hours he lay awake thinking of the man upstairs, the man who, uninvited, was sleeping under his roof.

He might have told Neel to turn him out of the house. But he didn't dare, fearing she might go with him. Indeed, there was every chance she would. Besides, if she once started talking . . .

On the other hand, he simply couldn't bear the thought of her going upstairs to join her Karl. He listened to her regular breathing. One of her hands was touching his shoulder.

What was that blonde doing in Sneek? And what was she hanging around in the Onder den Linden for?

He wasn't afraid. No, he wasn't afraid of anything. Certainly not of Karl. In fact, at one moment he was seriously tempted to go up and talk to him, then and there, just to see what he was like.

Why shouldn't he talk to the fellow? As things were . . .

All night long he never more than dozed, and next day the lack of sleep had a strange effect upon him. He had a feeling of emptiness, but at the same time of lightness. When he went into his office and put on his white coat, he wondered what was the use of it all. As in a dream, he opened the door to the waiting room and saw the old man with intercostal neutralgia, whom he'd been treating for two years.

"Good morning, Doctor... I'm afraid it's no better.... Last night I had to get up three times.... Lying down it's unbearable, and it looks as though I'll end up standing all night...."

"Let me see... How old are you?"

"Sixty-four... Getting on for sixty-five... And until these pains came on two years ago, I was..."

The old man started undressing, unnoticed by Kuperus, who was getting out his case book and his instruments. When the latter at last looked around, he was confronted by a bare, scraggy chest.

"You can put your clothes on again."

"Aren't you going to look at me?"

"I examined you two weeks ago."

"But I'm getting worse."

"Just so!"

"What do you mean?"

A bleak note of anxiety came into the old man's voice.

"You've had sixty-four years of life. It isn't everybody that has so much."

"You mean to say...?"

"That it's coming to an end...I'll give you a month....Go on, you can get dressed."

He'd had enough of all these people who were afraid of death! Wasn't he a sick man himself? Hadn't he been examined by a doctor in Amsterdam?

But that was *before*. Now, everything was changed. He no longer studied himself, no longer listened to the palpitations of his heart. He ate and drank everything that came his way, and indulged in nightly excesses.

There were tears in the old man's eyes. More disgusted than ever, the doctor pushed him out of the room.

"Next, please!"

He was no longer afraid of the writer of the anonymous letter. He thought quite a lot about that person, but only because it amused him to do so. It was like a riddle.

Was it Neel? Van Malderen? Someone he didn't know? He wanted to find out, to satisfy his curiosity. He scrutinized everyone who came near him, because he was convinced whoever it was would be anxious to see how he was taking it.

What really worried him were the other letters, the ones that had to be answered. There was one from his brother-in-law in Amsterdam, one from the aunt in Leeuwarden, and quite a number from Alice's friends.

Her disappearance had been reported in the papers, and people wrote to him for further details. The Amsterdam brother-in-law was annoyed because he thought the scandal might affect his career. He was a schoolmaster. He even accused Kuperus of having had it put in the papers on purpose.

As for the artificial blonde in the Onder den Linden, her presence in Sneek had been explained. She had confided in Van Malderen, whose appearance suited him for the role of father confessor.

She was named Lina. Schutter had been in the habit of sending her two hundred guilders a month, and now and again he spent a week with her in Amsterdam.

Then the money had stopped, and she'd come to Sneek to see about it. Now she had less than ever — not even enough to pay for her fare back to Amsterdam or her hotel bill, which was mounting up day by day!

"I think she's counting on one of us," said

Van Malderen. "She's not really a bad girl, you know, and if it wasn't for my wife..."

His face belied his words, and Kuperus was convinced Van Malderen had already fallen to her charms and was providing her with pocket money.

"Hello!...Is that you, Doctor?...I'm sorry to disturb you, and I'd better say right away that I don't want to raise any false hopes, but we've had news from London to say that a woman arrived at Dover yesterday wearing clothes similar to your wife's. She had no identity papers....Of course there may be nothing in it...."

It was the superintendent of police.

"Should I go there?" asked Kuperus in just the right tone of voice.

"Not at present. There'd be no point in it. I've asked for a photograph of the woman in question to be sent...."

It couldn't go on like that forever. The days passed. January gave place to February, and in the latter half of the month a slow thaw set in. It was just a question of time now. When the ice was gone, the bodies would come to the surface, and however deserted the spot might be, something was bound to be noticed, if only a bit of dress or overcoat.

Meanwhile, a meeting had taken place between Kuperus and Karl. The doctor had decided he really couldn't go on living in the house without seeing the face of the lodger.

One morning when Neel went down to light the kitchen fire and make the coffee, he went up to the attic on tiptoe and suddenly burst in.

And, sure enough, there was someone in the bed, a very young man, unshaven, who slowly opened his eyes. When he saw Kuperus, he didn't move, but a frown slowly gathered on his forehead.

"Excuse me," said the doctor automatically.

It was a silly thing to say, but he hadn't thought of anything else. He listened to Karl's breathing, then said:

"Are you ill?"

"A little," answered the other in German.

"Since when?"

"I stayed in bed all yesterday."

Kuperus felt his pulse, put his hand on his forehead.

"Influenza. Nothing more. But it could easily develop into bronchitis. Has Neel brought you up hot drinks?"

"Some grog."

"I suppose you're staying in bed today?"

"I think I better."

There was nowhere to sit except on the edge

of the bed, so that's where Kuperus installed himself.

"I understand you haven't been able to find work."

Karl merely sighed, as much as to say:

"What's the use of pretending. You know as well as I do that I'm not looking for work."

He was a nice-looking fellow. His features were well drawn and sensitive. His mouth had an ironical, even a sarcastic, twist. His clothes were in a heap on the floor.

"They haven't found your wife?"

"Not yet."

This time the doctor winced. He found the young man's eyes disconcerting.

"Why didn't you take any notice of Neel before? Why all of a sudden?"

"I didn't think about her."

"And of course there was your wife! She nearly found out about me once, but I said I'd come to read the gas meter."

There were a lot of things Kuperus hadn't known before that were now coming to light.

"I'll send you up some aspirin," he said, going to the door.

That was February 2. In the course of the morning Mme Costens called from Leeuwarden to ask if there was any further news of her niece. And then at eleven o'clock a policeman came to the door. The doctor was in the middle of his consultations, but he was urgently requested to come to the Town Hall.

Sending his patients away, he put on his fur coat and, with it, all his dignity. At the Town Hall they were waiting for him, the mayor, the superintendent of police, and two or three others, who shook his hand with unusual solemnity. He was asked to sit down.

"You must excuse us, Doctor.... We have a very painful task to perform, and you may be assured you have all our sympathy in the ordeal that's in store for you...."

He was pale that day, which happened to be just right.

"Your wife has been found.... Or, rather, I should say her body has...."

The mayor turned his eyes away, so forcibly did Kuperus, grim and rigid, give the impression of great suffering nobly borne. As a matter of fact, without his wanting it to, his mind had reverted to Karl.

"I'm afraid we must ask you to accompany us."

The canal had thawed. They went in the mayor's car toward Schutter's cottage, but they had to do the last part on foot, for fear the car would get stuck in the mud. As they approached, they saw two boats on the canal and a little group of people on the bank, standing near a small cart.

For the rest of the way, the mayor held Kuperus's arm affectionately.

"Courage, dear friend...I'd like to have spared you this, but you know how things are: you've got to identify the body."

The sky was dull and colorless except for a gap lit by a patch of sunshine. Though thawing, it was still cold. Underfoot was a slush of melting snow and mud. As they came up, the little crowd moved aside, and Kuperus could see on the cart a covered form that looked like a body.

Someone was shaking him by the hand. It was Moers, the police doctor, whom he knew well.

"Just a formality...I'm afraid there's no room for doubt."

He lifted up a corner of the tarpaulin. Kuperus stared glassily, without wincing. He was being held up on both sides, in case he fainted.

"My dear colleague, may I have a couple of words with you?"

Moers took him aside. Kuperus noticed that they were dragging the canal.

"Your wife was murdered....Before being thrown in the canal, she had already been killed by a revolver bullet in the chest...."

What would Neel say about it? And Karl?...
He'd had a funny way of talking that morning
about his wife's disappearance.

Next, it was the turn of the superintendent
to take him aside. Everybody turned to look at
them as they walked up and down.

"I'd better come to the point right away....
You've already shown great self-control....
The thing is, there's every likelihood of our
finding another body shortly....You must forgive me if I mention a name, but I have no
choice....A hat has been found, and the initials
in it are Schutter's....When you consider that
they both disappeared the same day...We're
dragging the canal...."

Kuperus said nothing. He wasn't expected
to say anything, and everyone was glad he
didn't. It was so much more dignified.

"The question will no doubt arise whether
this is a case of double suicide − for things like
that do happen, you know − or whether it's
one of murder....Perhaps you'd like to go
home now?"

"I'll stay until they finish searching."

And he stayed, walking up and down by himself, followed by inquisitive glances. A hundred times he passed within a yard of the cart
on which Alice's remains were laid.

He thought of nothing, or, rather, of nothing

79

in particular. His thoughts roamed all over. For instance, he recalled the arguments he'd had with Alice, who always said it was his fault they had no children, whereas he maintained it was hers. . . . He almost smiled at the recollection. . . .

Suppose he had a child with Neel?

He heard the voices of the boatmen as they went on dragging. At two o'clock a diver arrived. They screwed on his helmet, and a man worked the air pump.

A photographer came to take pictures of the scene for an Amsterdam paper. He was a local man, at whose shop Kuperus had his film developed.

The police visited the cottage and returned arguing hotly. One of them was sure there'd been a third person in the place; the others swore there'd been only two.

Kuperus looked at them as coldly as if he'd been called upon to perform a post-mortem on some unknown person.

The funniest thing was that the mayor sent his car back with a flask full of tea and some sandwiches for him.

FOUR

The mystery began suddenly and for no apparent reason. It seemed to condense out of nothing, like an autumn fog, and before he knew where he was, Kuperus was in the thick of it. There it was all around him, blotting out or distorting all reality, putting all human contacts out of focus.

It must have been about six o'clock. Kuperus was very tired, having spent the whole afternoon on his feet by the waterside. He was now following a canal, not the one by the cottage, but the one that ran in front of his house, where the quays were paved with flagstones.

It was still thawing fast. Drops trickled from every roof, and the reflections of the street lamps flickered once more on the rippling water.

He was getting near the house. He could already see the lighted window of the grocer's, which was only three doors away. In it were packs of chocolate and long sticks of macaroni tied by a red ribbon so they would stand up like a sheaf of corn.

Between the window and the shop was a low screen, so low that anyone inside could easily see over it into the street. There were three people in the shop, and as he passed, three pairs of eyes stared at him.

He took out his key and inserted it in the lock. As he did so a new question flashed into his mind:

What were they thinking?

He had already wondered what Neel might think, and Karl. Now for the first time he was concerned with the world at large, with the people in the street. . . .

What were they thinking?

Yes, what were they thinking about him, those three women in the shop? What were they saying about him, as they stood at the white marble counter doing their shopping or waiting to be served?

He shut the front door behind him, and paused with a frown in the outer hall, finding the house in darkness. He only had to switch the light on – it was done in a second – but he was nonetheless put out by the chilly reception.

For sixteen years he had been living in that house. He went up the three white stone steps and pushed open the glass-paneled door to the inner hall. There he stopped in front of the coat stand, beside which stood an umbrella stand made of imitation delft.

"Neel!" he called.

The little jar to his nerves he'd experienced on passing the grocer's turned into a vague uneasiness. The house seemed empty, dead. On the ground floor were two big rooms, the living room and dining room, then, beyond the stairs, the kitchen and laundry. A window at the back of the hall opened on a little whitewashed courtyard.

The waiting room and office were on the entresol, and up to that floor the red stair-carpet was covered with a strip of canvas, because few patients bothered to wipe their feet.

"Neel!"

There was no light in the kitchen, and Neel knew he didn't like her to go out shopping in the evening. He went into the living room, but stood there frowning, feeling out of place. The next moment, however, there was a noise upstairs, the slam of a door, then steps on the attic stairs.

When Neel came into the room, she was rather red and she looked hesitantly at the doctor.

"So, Madame is dead..." she said.

He nodded gravely, at the same time looking at her intently, asking himself the same question as before:

What would Neel think?

"Where were you?" he asked.

"In my room. I was giving Karl a cup of tea."

"And you told him, I suppose?"

She didn't say no. Neel must have heard about it from the people next door or from tradesmen coming to the house.

So she and Karl had been talking it over! On an impulse, he decided to make an experiment. He walked rapidly up to her without giving the least hint of what he was going to do.

She watched him approach without any sign of surprise. She allowed him to caress her, merely saying:

"How could you think of that...now?"

The important thing was that she hadn't shrunk from his touch.

But what did that prove? Did it prove anything? Couldn't she have remained as calm as that even if she thought him a murderer?

"Get my dinner ready..."

She seemed relieved as she went out, but that certainly didn't prove anything either, since she always seemed relieved when she left him.

How could he know? And not only with her,

but with all the others?

Schutter's body had been found just as the light began to fail. The absence of his wallet was noticed immediately. An inquiry was opened.

He tried again next day, with one of his patients, a fat woman who sold cheese and who had a wen. Before opening the door to her, he deliberately set his features into a stony stare. He treated her brusquely, almost roughly.

And all the time he watched her carefully, asking himself:

Is she afraid of me?

She wasn't. Not in the least. Only rather surprised. She didn't seem to understand, or she may have thought he was ill himself.

"I won't be seeing any patients tomorrow or the next day, because of the funeral...."

"Oh, I'm so sorry. Has there been a death in the family?"

She didn't even know!

Drawing a blank with her did not discourage him, however. He tried with the others. His manner became stiff and jerky, his speech curt. Suddenly he would look keenly, fiercely into their eyes to ferret out their secret thoughts.

The brother-in-law came from Amsterdam, and the aunt from Leeuwarden, and a few other relations, one of whom was a weedy young man with a red nose who was already in mourning for his father and who had such a bad cold that he looked all the time as though he'd been crying.

Kuperus had been before the examining magistrate, his friend Anton Groven, who received him with great cordiality and many apologies, after which he asked him a few questions of minor importance.

"Now that the post-mortem's over, there's no reason why the funeral shouldn't take place. . . ."

Kuperus had bought a new black suit and overcoat, and had a band of crepe put around his hat. The undertakers came and fixed up the living room for the occasion. The coffin was brought, candles lit, the doorbell muffled with a bit of cloth, and the front door left ajar so that visitors could come and go freely.

The brother-in-law stayed the night, but the aunt went back to her fish store, to return next day for the funeral.

Alice Kuperus came from an Amsterdam family and was a Catholic. A mass was arranged.

That night Neel put her foot down.

"No! Not when Madame is lying there. . ."

Kuperus looked her in the eyes.

"Then you won't sleep with Karl either!"

He was jealous! There was no getting away from the fact. There were three bedrooms on the second floor, and he forced her to sleep in the vacant one. Moreover, he got up twice during the night to make sure she hadn't given him the slip.

His brother-in-law, waking, opened his door. "What's the matter?"

Standing barefoot, in his nightshirt, Kuperus answered:

"Can't you sleep?"

"What about you?"

"Never mind about me."

If his strangeness was put on, it was also in a way sincere. He *had* to act queerly. He *had* to watch for the effect on other people.

Some were bound to suspect him. That was inevitable. The local paper, of course, made the most of the missing wallet, suggesting robbery as the motive. But how could anyone fail to see that there might be another one?

The examining magistrate would no doubt have discussed the matter with the police and the public prosecutor. Was Kuperus being watched? Perhaps, unknown to him, an exhaustive inquiry was going on all around him.

"Did you meet anybody when you went out shopping?" he asked Neel.

"No. What do you mean?"

"Nothing."

He had meant the police. They'd get detectives over from Amsterdam for a case like this. And in order not to put him on his guard, wasn't it natural that they would get hold of Neel in the street or in a shop?

Alice's sister came only on the day of the funeral. She was expecting a baby. She was the living image of Alice, but five years younger. Kuperus was particularly preoccupied with her. Wasn't she the most likely person to suspect something? Yet he wasn't able to detect the faintest sign of it. She had greeted him exactly as usual, kissing him on both cheeks, as they did in the family, shedding a few tears as she murmured:

"Who would ever have thought!..."

This wasn't quite an ordinary funeral. The words that were generally spoken at funerals would in this case have sounded out of place. Prolonged silent handshakes were the order of the day.

For how were people to say:

"Poor woman!..."

Or:

"What a terrible mishap!..."

Or:

"And in the prime of life!..."

She had gone off with another man. Her dishonor was public knowledge. It was the first time anything like it had happened in Sneek. It was a subject that couldn't be broached in front of children, and Alice's sister had left her boy of seven at home for fear he would hear something unsuited to his young ears.

For the same reason, the priest had suggested that the service be as simple as possible.

There were lots of people. A long procession of black clothes and umbrellas following the hearse. But it was a cold group, with dry eyes. They came because it was their duty to, not to show approval.

At every window, as they passed, peering eyes watched Kuperus, who held himself very erect and stared back, instead of keeping his eye on the coffin, as people usually do.

No flowers, of course! No wreaths or crosses!

The next day there was much the same crowd following the remains of Cornelius de Schutter, with the addition of two very elegant women, cousins from Amsterdam, who had brought their lawyer with them.

The evening of the funeral Kuperus, after going to the station with the relatives, appeared at the Onder den Linden, where he wasn't expected, to say the least.

There was a dead silence as he shook hands

all around. Then he called out to Willem:

"A gin and bitters, please."

It was the same here as it was at home. The house he had lived in for sixteen years seemed suddenly to have changed – or, rather, it seemed to have died. There was no longer any reason, for instance, why an object should be where it was rather than anywhere else, and it now appeared incredible that he and Alice could have argued, fussed, and fretted over just how the rooms should be arranged.

And now the same feeling assailed him in the Onder den Linden. For years and years he had been going there. He had his favorite corner, his own billiard cue secured by a little padlock, and his name on the list of members of the committee.

It was in a slightly contemptuous tone that he asked:

"Well? What's the news?"

"We must have an election," sighed Van Malderen.

"Ah! Yes . . ."

He looked up at the list and suddenly remembered his decision.

"Who's standing?" he asked.

Somebody would have to be elected president in Schutter's place.

"Nobody's come forward yet. . . . I daresay

Pijpekamp may. . . ."

"Pijpekamp? Why, he can't make a break of fifty!" objected Kuperus.

"It's he who provides the prize every year."

"Only because he sells such things!"

"Who else is there?"

He drank his gin in a single swallow, threw back his head, and looked challengingly at his fellow members one after the other.

"Well. . . Why shouldn't I put *my* name forward?"

The question was received in stony silence. Loos was the only one to make any response, and he raised his eyebrows. Kuperus turned on him.

"What do you mean by that, Loos?" he asked. "Have you any objection to my standing? If you have, out with it! If there's one thing I can't put up with, it's people who don't say what they really think."

He was almost trembling. He felt he was on the verge of finding out what he wanted to know.

"You're taking it the wrong way," stammered Loos awkwardly. "I didn't mean it that way at all. But considering that you're in mourning. . ."

"I don't see why that should stop me from playing billiards."

"On the contrary. It's just the thing to do.

It'll take your mind off other things."

So there it was! He was now a candidate for the presidency of the club. He was asking to be the elected successor to Cornelius de Schutter.

That night he couldn't help saying to Neel: "They're going to make me president of the club."

Of course she couldn't understand what it meant, but he'd said it just the same!

As for the anonymous letter, no one came forward. Nevertheless, somebody had written it. Somewhere in Holland, somewhere in Sneek no doubt (he hadn't thought at the time of looking at the postmark) was a person who knew, a person who could at any moment go to the examining magistrate and say:

"The man who murdered Schutter and Mme Kuperus is..."

Well? Why didn't he do so?

He could also come and ring the doctor's bell and be shown into the living room or the office. He could smile at the doctor and drop a few hints. He could play with him like a cat with a mouse, until he finally let fall:

"Look here, Doctor, I wonder if you could let me have a thousand guilders..."

Or two thousand, or even five! He could ask

for whatever he liked: to come and stay in the house, for instance, and sleep in the best bedroom with Neel. He could have all his meals there. . . .

Nobody had come forward, at least not in that sort of way. But what was there to prove that it wasn't Neel? Or Van Malderen, or Loos, who had raised his eyebrows? Lastly, why not Karl? He had only Neel's word for it that the German had been there only five months.

Karl had recovered from his influenza. Twice Kuperus had asked Neel:

"Has he found a job yet?"

To which she had simply answered:

"No."

Her tone obviously meant to say that he had not even considered looking for one.

Suppose his presence in the house was noticed. Wouldn't it be awkward? What explanation could Kuperus give? He couldn't very well say that he was giving him shelter because he was in love with the maid.

"I must have a talk with him, Neel."

"He's gone out. I don't know when he'll be back."

"He must leave the house, Neel. In fact, he must leave today."

She waited, guessing there was something to follow.

"I'm prepared to give him a hundred guilders. With that, he can go and look for a job in Amsterdam or Rotterdam, or anywhere he likes on the other side of the Zuider Zee. If he doesn't find one at once, I'll send him a little more. . . ."

"I'll tell him."

If Karl refused, would that prove anything? For a long time he turned the question over in his mind, finally deciding that it wouldn't be any indication at all, one way or the other. In the evening Neel brought his answer:

"He's catching the eleven o'clock train."

Kuperus was undecided whether to see him or not. In the end, he decided not to, and gave Neel the hundred guilders. Soon after, he heard steps on the stairs and then someone shutting the front door.

"Neel!" he shouted over the banister. "Come up, will you?"

He turned her head toward the light and looked in her eyes.

"Are you sad to see him go?"

"A little."

"Did you really love him?"

"It's difficult to say."

"And if he loved you, why was he willing to go?"

"There was no help for it."

"Get undressed. From now on, I don't want

you to have an affair with anyone, do you understand?...Nobody but me!"

The blood rose to his head, and for the time being nothing in the world mattered but Neel's passive body and her unfeeling eyes.

"Do you hate me, Neel?"

"No."

"Why not?"

"I don't know."

"Are you afraid of me?"

"Not that either."

He was wildly passionate. She might well have said, as on the first night:

"You're pretty hot stuff!"

He gazed into her gray eyes and racked his brain for something to say that might trouble their indifference.

"Neel!"

"Yes."

"Aren't you afraid of living here alone with me?"

"Why?"

"Aren't you?" he insisted.

"No."

"Neel."

"Yes."

"Are there any people suggesting that I killed my wife and Schutter?"

He still had her in his arms.

"Answer me. You needn't be afraid."

"There are."

"What do they say?"

"That you never can tell."

"And what else?"

"That it's bound to affect your practice."

"Go on."

"That you always were a bit odd."

Kuperus greeted the last remark with a harsh, raucous laugh. It was untrue, utterly untrue. People could only be fools to say a thing like that, or, if they weren't fools, they must be quite blind.

The truth was the exact opposite. The whole of his life, that is to say the whole of his first life, had been commonplace. He had been a perfectly ordinary Dutchman, like hundreds, like thousands of others, a doctor like any other doctor, a husband like any other husband.

His chief concern had always been to avoid anything that might single him out, make him seem original.

Wasn't his house in every way typical of a man of his means and social standing? Yes, and everything in it down to the last bit of bric-a-brac on the living-room mantelpiece. The meals served in it had always been exactly what everyone would expect to find in a middle-class household in Holland.

If he'd gone to Spitzbergen, it hadn't been with any idea of breaking out. On the contrary. It had been a cruise organized for the medical profession at specially reduced rates. There had been three hundred doctors on board.

He had been to Paris, but only on the occasion of an exposition, and that time, too, with a group.

And now they had the cheek to suggest that he'd always been odd! It just showed how people judged! Those same people who eyed him as he passed and whom he, too, watched closely, eager to catch the least hint of their thoughts...

"And you, Neel?...What do you think yourself?"

"I don't."

"What do you think of me?"

"Look out! You're hurting me."

"Are you going to stay here all your life?"

"I don't know."

Why was he haunted all the time by the idea that Neel might leave him?

"Well, I mean you to stay here, do you understand?...I'll pay you what you like, but I won't allow you to go....And what's more: I forbid you to speak to any other man!..."

"I'll have to speak to the butcher and the grocer."

"Fool!"

He still didn't know. She was so close to him, and yet no power on earth could drag from her what was going on behind that obstinate forehead.

"Look at me, Neel!"

"You're always asking me to look at you."

"Because I've got to know, sooner or later, what you think."

"Haven't I told you that I don't think anything at all?"

He went to sleep, exhausted, and woke up with a violent headache. He tried to shake off his obsession, but to no avail. He couldn't escape from this twilight that surrounded him, this emptiness, this absence of life, in which his own faltered like a flame deprived of air.

In a strange sort of way, he seemed to have become detached from things. He turned on his own axis in a hollow universe. He touched things without seeming to come really into contact with them; he spoke to people who no longer belonged to the same world as his.

Even in the café! His name had been put up. The members of the club had said nothing – at least not in front of him – and it had been decided that, since he was set on it, he should be elected president to succeed Schutter.

But nobody had congratulated him. Nobody had come forward to shake him by the hand.

And he couldn't help noticing that, though nobody ever refused to play with him, neither did anybody ever invite him to a game.

Far from taking the hint, he made a point of asking them all in turn. He stood rounds of drinks regardless of the cost. Money, like everything else, had lost its meaning.

What did it matter if he squandered it? As for Lina, they never spoke to him about her, and it was only by overhearing chance remarks that he learned anything.

Some said it was Van Malderen who had paid her hotel bill; others, that Loos had contributed, too, though without the lawyer's knowledge.

In any case, when Schutter's heirs had arrived, the two cousins from Amsterdam, Lina had turned up at the house and claimed a share of the estate equivalent to the allowance she had been receiving. It had ended with a hand-to-hand fight in which one of the cousins had got her dress torn!

Lina was still in Sneek, still subsidized by Van Malderen, and, according to some, by Loos also. But she had been forbidden by one or the other – or perhaps by both – to set foot in the Onder den Linden. She had left the hotel and was tucked away in a furnished room somewhere or other.

Why didn't they talk to Kuperus about her openly? He began to detest the whole lot of them. Certainly he despised them, and it was to gratify his contempt that he greeted them with an aggressive stare and forced them to shake hands with him.

He was even deliberately disagreeable, and no one dared say anything.

When the time came to make his inaugural speech as president, he flouted the traditions of the club in making no reference whatever to his predecessor. And at the end he suddenly took it into his head to declare:

"I trust that the honor you are conferring upon me is only the prelude to a career of public service. The next election is due in two years' time, and I would like to take this opportunity of announcing that it is my ambition to represent my fellow citizens of Sneek in Parliament. . . ."

The clapping, when he sat down, was perfunctory. And all the while, he scrutinized the faces around him, particularly the eyes, eyes that would not give up their secret.

For after all, people must think something! They must have some opinion about him and about the deaths of Alice and Schutter.

Did they think him a murderer, or didn't they? That was what he wanted to know! And if they didn't think it, were they too scared of him to say so?

As regards the second question, the answer seemed to be yes. He became more convinced of it every day. They were afraid of him, every one of them.

Even the examining magistrate, Anton Groven! Twice Kuperus went to see him without being summoned. He called him by his Christian name and offered him a cigarette, which the other hadn't the courage to refuse. And all Groven could find to say was:

"We haven't dropped the case, though I can't say we're making much headway. . . . It may be we never shall. . . . "

Suppose they arrested him? From time to time Kuperus came back to that question. What would they do to him? What would he do about it himself?

At one time there had been no doubt about what he'd have done. Rather than spend ten or twenty years in prison, he'd have put a bullet into his head.

Not now! Why shouldn't he go to prison? Why should he be any worse off there than anywhere else? There was only one thing that upset that idea: to know that Neel would be free. . . .

Unless of course. . . And why not? . . . Rather

101

than allow her to share the bed of other masters, whom she would look at placidly, with her pale indifferent eyes...rather than that, he might kill her, too, before they arrested him. He'd have the courage; he didn't doubt that for a moment. And with that done, he could go to prison without a worry in the world.

He turned the idea over in his mind as he walked through the streets. Like other people, he stopped and looked into shop windows, but without interrupting his train of thought.

Yes, it was really quite simple when you came to think of it....

"Neel!" he called, as he went indoors.

She came from the laundry, her hands covered with soapsuds, since it was washing day.

"Neel! I've been thinking about you, and I've made a decision."

"What?"

"I can't tell you....But you may as well know this much: that it's only today that I've realized how much attached I am to you."

She answered merely with a slight shrug of her shoulders. The next moment another wild idea had come into his head. Until the last few days, he had reflected before doing anything. He had avoided doing or saying anything on the spur of the moment. It was different now. An idea no sooner came into his mind than he acted on it. The more absurd the idea was, the more certain was he to come out with it.

"You're doing the washing, are you?"

"Yes."

"For the last time . . . Tomorrow we'll see about getting another maid."

"What for?"

"To do the work. Then you'll be able to take it easy."

"Don't talk such nonsense. . . ."

She turned away, muttering, and he wasn't quite sure of the rest of the sentence, but it sounded something like:

"If you think that would do you any good, you're very much mistaken."

She was right there, and he knew it. It was one thing to have an affair with his servant, quite another to advertise it. If he did that, he would never be forgiven. But what did he care? Not a scrap. He didn't care about anything now. . . . Except for just one thing: to know what people thought about him.

And that was just what he couldn't find out. . . .

The winter was coming to an end, and boys began once again to play in the street. Near the lamppost ten yards from the doctor's front door was a slight drop in the level of the sidewalk, and there, for generations, boys had been in the habit of playing marbles.

One afternoon, Kuperus went out as usual to make his rounds, carrying his little bag and wearing the black overcoat he had bought when he went into mourning. He was wondering which of his patients he would begin with, and so engrossed was he by the question that for a moment he didn't see the boys.

Then suddenly he heard a loud whisper:

"Look out!...Here he comes...."

One boy was quite close to him, bending over his marbles. He looked around sharply, then quickly darted aside, flattening himself against the wall to let the doctor pass. Kuperus noticed his red scarf and a scar he had on his forehead.

The doctor had stopped dead. And the boys stood still, too, as though petrified, looking at him. For a few seconds not a movement was made on either side. It was as though life hung in suspense.

Then all at once the little boy with the red scarf was seized with panic. He took to his heels, and the others followed.

Why? What were they frightened of? What had their parents been saying to them?

Kuperus walked on, but a moment later he couldn't help turning around, and he saw the boys in a huddle at the corner, watching him cautiously.

FIVE

Everything was ready, and the doctor walked to and fro between the living room and the dining room, occasionally glancing at himself in the mirror over the mantelpiece.

Half an hour before, Neel had closed the shutters, assisted by Beetje, a girl of sixteen, too fat for her age, who, moreover, squinted. It was Neel who had engaged her and explained her duties. Kuperus rarely saw her, but her presence in the house made a great difference, because Neel was now always clean and neat in her black dress and white apron.

The dining-room clock struck five. It was a handsome clock, which struck the quarter hours. Kuperus had bought it on the occasion of his marriage.

He sat down in one of the armchairs in the dining room, then got up again to help himself to a cigar from the box that was already lying open on the table. He checked the impulse, however, remembering that it was not correct to receive your guests smoking a cigar.

The next moment a sarcastic smile came to his lips. He had remembered something else! That things of that sort no longer mattered. And, choosing a cigar, he bit the end off and lit it. What on earth did he care whether Mme Malderen was offended or not?

As a matter of fact, she probably wouldn't even notice, since she was inured to the smell of cigar smoke. Then why had he always made a point of not smoking while waiting for his guests to arrive?

Why? Because of his wife...Well, no! That wasn't true, and he had to admit it. He had always been as punctilious as she was in matters of etiquette.

It had been a regular thing for years for the Van Malderens to come to tea on Thursday, and once a month they stayed on for dinner. After the tragedy, Kuperus hadn't even thought about it, but he had been reminded of it a few days previously by Van Malderen, who, in the Onder den Linden, had said to him, a little awkwardly:

"Look here, Hans!...My wife's very cross with you."

"Why?"

"She says you've dropped her."

So now they were coming once again, Franz

106

with his somewhat heavy humor, Jane with her inquisitiveness, her ferrety eyes, which pried into every corner.

She was a flat-chested, swarthy little thing, and it would have been impossible to have found another like her in the whole of Friesland. In height, she was positively tiny, a whole head and shoulders shorter than her husband.

Kuperus went over to the stove, which was a huge thing built of dark-colored glazed tiles with brass fittings. He picked up the bottle of Burgundy that was warming up at the side, and felt it critically.

Two trays were ready on the table, just as they had always been in the days of Madame Kuperus. On one were the teacups, with toast, honey, and jam; on the other, the big wine glasses of cut glass and the box of cigars.

And suddenly, for the first time in his life, Kuperus did a thing that was really outrageous, so much so that he couldn't help once more looking at himself in the mirror. Without waiting any longer for his guests, he poured himself a full glass of wine. Then, sitting down to the left of the stove, he crossed his legs and began to sip it.

A glass of wine in one hand, a cigar in the other, its smoke swirling in a cloud around the pink silk lampshade! And already the room had begun to be impregnated with the characteristic smell of those Thursday teas, a blend of the Puerto Rican cigar with the slightly warm wine and the permanent smell of the linoleum and floor polish.

The bell rang. Neel went to open the door. The doctor could hear Franz saying something as he gave his coat and hat to the maid, then Jane's shrill voice asking:

"I hope we're not too early. Has the doctor finished his work?"

Then steps... The door opening... Jane Van Malderen running up to Kuperus and giving him a little peck on the cheek...

"My poor Hans... How are you getting on?"

And he answering coldly:

"Admirably, thanks!"

The two men shook hands, while Jane, looking around, exclaimed:

"Everything's just as it was. It makes me feel quite funny... to see all these things...."

She looked at the two trays, at the mantelpiece.

"Tell me, are you being properly looked after? It's terrible for a man to be all alone. I know if I'm away three days, the servants do absolutely nothing.... As a matter of fact, Neel seems to have changed. She seems neater and nicer-looking...."

Van Malderen had sat down with a sigh, knowing that his wife could go on chattering like that for an hour at a stretch.

"Shall I ring for the tea, Hans?"

"Do."

"You've changed, too, Hans. How shall I put it?...There's something more manly about you....they told me you'd aged, but to my mind you're better as you are...."

Neel came in with the teapot, and Kuperus managed to tread on her foot, just for fun, just to have contact with her.

"Thank you, my little Neel," he said.

He was well aware that his familiarity would shock Mme Van Malderen. That's why he'd said it. He wanted to awake her suspicions. He even toyed with the idea of saying straight out that Neel was his mistress. As soon as she was gone, Jane went on:

"I hope she doesn't take too many liberties now that Alice is no longer here."

On pronouncing Alice's name, Jane reddened, and she made haste to add:

"Forgive me, my poor Hans...I know I ought not to remind you...."

But he looked at her calmly, sipping his wine. In the living room the chandelier was not lit. That, too, was a tradition. It was by way of being a mark of special favor, of intimacy, that the Van Malderens were received, not in the living room, but in the dining room, which was considered cozier, chiefly because the stove gave out more heat. Between the folding doors, the living room was visible, bathed in a gentle half-light.

Jane sighed and blew her nose.

"I was thinking of the last time we were here.... Who would ever have thought... You must have been terribly unhappy, Hans!"

Her husband sighed again. Perhaps he foresaw the inevitable scene. Leaning back in his chair, he gazed at the pink lampshade.

"You were such a close couple.... Yes, you were. I used to say so to Franz every Thursday as we went home.... It was a great misfortune that you never had any children."

To startle her, he said, looking at his cigar ash:

"It's not too late."

"Oh, Hans!"

"What do you mean, 'Oh, Hans'? Do you think I'm too old to have children?"

"Don't say such things... And here of all places! With Alice's photograph looking at us!"

It was true. A small photograph he no longer noticed, so used was he to seeing it in its place. It had been taken in Paris, because Alice had thought it would be done better there than anywhere else. They'd had an argument about that. He maintained that Paris was a very much overrated place, that the town itself was dirty and the women too made-up.

"You might just as well have your photograph taken in Sneek, where it'll be just as well done at half the price."

No. She had insisted on Paris, and had returned with a photograph that was commonplace enough. And there it stood in a silver frame beside other family photographs.

From her nose, Jane Van Malderen's handkerchief passed to her eyes.

"How did you hear about it, Hans?"

"Hear about what?"

He looked at her sternly, aggressively. That was his way of looking at people nowadays, as though he meant to frighten them.

"You know very well what I mean!"

"Oh, yes," he sneered. "You mean how did I find out that she was deceiving me with our excellent friend Schutter!"

"Hans!"

"What?"

"She's dead!"

"And what about it?"

"Whatever she did wrong, she's paid for it. . . . And knowing Alice as I did, I can't bring myself to believe she was as guilty as all that. . . .

Who knows? Perhaps it was the first time...
just a moment's aberration..."

"What do you think of this Burgundy, Franz?
Don't you think it's just a little corky?"

For a few moments there was silence, which
gave Mme Van Malderen an opportunity to fill
her little rodent's mouth with buttered toast.

Suddenly she jumped up and ran over to a
little table, returning with a ball of pale blue
wool and a little rectangle of knitting.

"It was I who taught her that stitch. Only
the week before..." said Jane, gazing at the
wool, which was really of the most angelic color.
"She was going to make a little sweater for indoors.... That was just before the cold weather
came.... And then when the frost came..."

"She was under the ice," put in Kuperus.

Even Franz started. He sat up in his chair
and stared at his friend with an expression of
alarm, while Jane exclaimed:

"It's simply dreadful!"

"It was simply dreadful when they pulled
them out! Would you believe it: Schutter's
body was almost torn in two by the grapnel.
One side of his face was ripped right open...."

"Oh, do stop! For heaven's sake!"

"I didn't begin it."

"Let me tell you something, Hans."

"If you like."

112

"I think I know you well enough. We've known each other for twelve years. In fact, you and Alice have been our only really intimate friends. . . . You've been brooding too much over your sorrow, Hans. . . . Yes, yes. I know you have. I've been watching you every day as you passed."

Her house had a sort of closed-in veranda where she spent most of the day, keeping an eye on everything that happened in the street.

"You know, Hans, people turn around to look at you as you pass. There's something so strange about you. . . . You're nursing your sorrow, that's what it is, instead of throwing it off. . . . I was saying so only last week, wasn't I, Franz? . . . And it was then I thought that I ought to come and give you some advice. . . ."

Kuperus looked at her without turning a hair, but Van Malderen seemed more and more ill at ease.

"You know our one thought is to help you, don't you, Hans? Well, I've come to tell you that you ought to go away for a while."

For a moment he was taken aback, though he didn't show it. But his features set a little harder, and he bit into the end of his cigar.

"You ought to go away for a good long holiday. Go to Switzerland or the South of France. . . . Or why not Italy? . . . I know you can afford it,

113

and it'll take your mind off all this trouble...."

She paused for a moment, drank a mouthful of tea, then rattled on, staring at the tablecloth:

"And you might even come across some young person – a young widow would be best, don't you think so, Franz?...You've no idea what it costs me to say such a thing – I was so fond of Alice – but at your age life's not over...."

"You haven't got someone up your sleeve already?" he asked, and nobody could possibly have told whether he was joking or not.

"No, I haven't," stammered Jane. "And, in any case, I think someone from elsewhere would be much more suitable. Someone with whom you can make a fresh start."

Kuperus had his eyes half shut. It was hot. The Burgundy had inflamed his cheeks, and the fire in the stove was roaring, as in the Onder den Linden. From time to time a truck passed along the street, or a motor barge on the canal would sound a blast on its horn for the swing bridge to be opened.

A few feet in front of him he could see Jane Van Malderen's irregular features, her scraggy neck, the cameo that hung around it. On his left, he was conscious of her husband, from whom drifted a cloud of cigar smoke.

But it was rather vague, rather blurred, deliberately so. The lights in the house were heavily shaded, with pink silk in the dining room, with yellow silk in the living room.

The upholstery was dingy, a mixture of every color of the rainbow, but faded until it was completely nondescript.

Everything seemed dim, soft, and neutral.... He forgot for a moment that something was changed, and in his mind's eye he could see Alice sitting beside Jane with some work in her lap, talking in an undertone so as not to disturb the conversation of the men.

He could remember that when he was in the middle of a discussion with Franz, he would suddenly be conscious of Alice's voice saying:

"Three plain and one purl. Is that it?"

And Jane would take her knitting and look at it and...

But that was all over and done with now. And what were they after, these two? What had they come for? He knew now. It hadn't taken Jane long to give her little game away. They wanted to persuade him to go away!

He was to be eliminated. Driven from the town. Franz hadn't said anything himself. Of course not! Everybody knew that when there was anything disagreeable to be done he'd always get his wife to do it. Only this time, she'd been a little too precipitate.

With a sigh, Kuperus got up from his chair, threw the end of his cigar into the coal scuttle, and lit another. His attitude was becoming more aggressive. So far he had left the initiative to Jane. Now it was obvious he was going to take the offensive himself.

"What do they say?" he asked, standing in front of her.

"Who? What do you mean?"

"I'm asking you what people are saying about me in town. You're not going to pretend they say nothing, are you? This is the first time in thirty years that anything so dramatic has happened in Sneek. . . ."

Thirty years before there'd been a murder of two little girls.

"There's been nothing like it for thirty years," he went on. "Schutter, the richest man in town, the best connected, the most popular, has been murdered at the same time as the wife of Dr. Kuperus."

"Please, Hans!"

"Is there any reason why I shouldn't speak about it? I should have thought I was the person most entitled to! And it is made obvious to everybody that the unfortunate Dr. Kuperus has been made a fool of by his wife. . . ."

"How can you talk like that?"

"I said made a fool of. . . . And, once more, if

anyone has a right to say that, it's me!...Now tell me: What do people say about it all?"

Van Malderen fidgeted in his chair, while his wife began, timidly:

"What do you expect us to say, Hans?... We're terribly sorry for you...."

"That's not true."

"What do you mean, it's not true?"

"No one's ever sorry for a man who's been made ridiculous...."

"Sorrow isn't ridiculous."

"Suppose I don't feel any sorrow?"

"You're not yourself, Hans....When you think it over, you'll see I'm right. I know you will. You'll see there's only one thing to do: go right away and forget all about it."

"Well, I won't."

"Why not?"

"Because you all want me to."

"What's that got to do with it?"

"Only that I'm not going to toe the line... And now you might as well tell me what people say. Do they think I knew my wife was carrying on with Schutter?"

"Really!"

"Answer me."

"I've never heard anyone suggest such a thing."

He knew perfectly well what he was leading

up to. He might have stopped at that. He'd already gone far enough. But he didn't want to stop. He was standing, his head level with the hanging lamp that shone on the embroidered tablecloth. And the bit of blue knitting was lying on the table, exactly as though Alice would be picking it up at any moment to go on with it.

"Who do the police suspect?"

"How should I know?"

"Why can't you leave her alone, Hans?" said Van Malderen.

"Then answer for her."

"Nobody knows anything. What do you expect people to say?"

"The less people know, the more they talk. . . . Come on, what do they say?"

"That it's the work of some vagrant."

His nerves were stretched to breaking point. He would have liked to have done with it once and for all. Done with what? With this gnawing anguish, this impatience, this giddiness, this nameless uneasiness.

"And me?"

"What about you?"

"I might have killed them myself. Hasn't anybody suggested that yet?"

"Stop, Hans!" pleaded Jane. "Stop, or I'll go."

She was dabbing her eyes with her handkerchief. Her breast was heaving with emotion.

"Let's talk of something else," she went on. "If I'd known it would come to this..."

Calmly Kuperus pursued the subject.

"For my part, I'm quite sure there are people who suspect me and don't hesitate to say so."

"What does it matter to you what they say?"

Kuperus stood his ground stolidly, and the others didn't even notice that this last remark had hit him like a stone. For a moment he could find nothing to say, could not even lift his cigar to his lips. Finally, he said very quietly:

"You're right. It makes no difference to me at all."

"Listen, Hans," broke in Van Malderen, "we've all been trying to help you, and it was to show our affection and our confidence in you that we elected you president of the club...."

At the mention of the club Kuperus regained all his aggressiveness.

"Only because I forced you to," he countered.

"You were elected unanimously."

"On a show of hands. Nobody had the courage to refuse, but I don't mind betting they're sorry now."

"You're very unjust.... And you're making it

119

very difficult for us. . . . Do you think we can't see that you're in a bad way? If you don't do something about it, it'll end up badly. . . . I've been watching you in the Onder den Linden. Jane's been watching you as you walk along the street. We hear what your friends say about you. . . ."

"So you're coming to the point at last!"

"I wish it hadn't been necessary."

Van Malderen got up in turn and stood with his hands clasped under his coattails.

"You can't fail to be aware that your practice has dwindled. Doesn't that mean anything to you?"

It was a fact. In a few weeks, half the doctor's patients had faded away.

"You know the Frieslanders as well as I do, and most of all those of Sneek. . . . The people here have a horror of scandal. So much so that they feel it reflects on them if they even set foot in the house of a woman . . ."

"Who has been unfaithful to her husband."

"Since you want me to say it − yes . . . And if you had a son, he'd find his schoolmates turning their backs on him. . . ."

"As the whole town is going to turn its back on me − is that what you mean?"

"Nobody blames you. . . . On the contrary, we're all sorry for you. . . ."

"And I don't care whether anyone's sorry for me or not."

He said it airily, as though he was thoroughly pleased with himself.

"I tell you I don't care! I don't care two hoots for the Billiard Club, nor for my practice, nor for any young widows who might be waiting for me in Switzerland!"

Jane was completely bewildered. She gave a meaning look at her husband, jerking her head toward the bottle. No doubt she thought Kuperus was drunk.

"You'd never understand that. All you're concerned with is your petty reputations in this petty little town. I don't mind betting Jane took an hour to get ready to come here, and I daresay she even went to the hairdresser's this morning, so as to be properly dolled up for the occasion!...A lot of good it's done her!... But it had to be done. Just because it always has been."

He opened the door and shouted across the hall:

"Neel! Bring another bottle, will you, my precious!"

Turning back into the room, he looked at Alice's photograph, which he picked up.

"In her time, it would have seemed very uncalled for to produce a second bottle of wine.

'Really, Hans! What are you thinking of? People will be taking us for drunkards!'...What a lot of nonsense. All for the sake of a pack of fools..."

"Hans!" pleaded Jane once again.

" 'Hans! Hans!' " He imitated her high-pitched voice. "You won't get anywhere with your 'Hans! Hans!' Hans doesn't care a damn for you, and he's not going to Switzerland or the South of France or anywhere else just to oblige the townsfolk of Sneek, who are beginning to be scared of him!"

He stopped, surprised himself by what he had said. He looked narrowly at the others, but they made no sign. Neel came in with another bottle of Burgundy, and as she uncorked it he patted her thigh familiarly.

After shutting the door, he came back to his guests, running his hand across his forehead.

"What were we saying? Won't you sit down again? It's not time for you to go yet. Don't forget: it's half past six you're supposed to go, except on the second Thursday of the month, when you have dinner thrown in...."

Jane turned toward her husband.

"Franz!...Do say something...Stop him... Don't let him drink any more."

Kuperus poured himself a glass of wine, which, having come straight from the cellar, was cold and sharp.

"Look here, Hans! Do be reasonable. . ."

"No."

Jane had been blowing her nose until it was red, a tiny little button nose that now looked like an unripe cherry.

"At first you behaved with great dignity, and everybody was grateful to you for it."

"Thanks."

"We'd better go now. . . . Think over what we've said, and remember that we only said it out of affection for you. . . ."

"Thanks again."

"Come on, Jane. Are you ready?"

She nodded and moved toward the door. Halfway there, however, she turned around to say:

"I can't bear leaving you like this. . . . And I can't help thinking. . ."

"That I'll do something rash? You needn't worry. As soon as you're gone, I'll call Neel, and we'll chat quietly till it's time for us to go to bed. . . . You see how things are. You're the first people to be told officially, but I'm sure the neighbors have a pretty shrewd idea by now. . . . For the last few days she's even been having her meals with me. It makes a little company for me. You see, I'm not used to eating alone. . . ."

"Let's go, Franz!"

And Jane fled. She was in such a hurry that she put her arm in the wrong sleeve of her coat. It was a coat she had modeled on one of Alice's, except that Alice's was cinnamon, whereas hers was blue-gray.

"Shall I see you tomorrow?" asked Franz, holding out his hand.

"Tomorrow and every other day... To my mind, the president of a club ought to be regular in his attendance. So until you throw me out..."

"Nonsense!"

"Good-bye, good night, sleep well!...As a matter of fact, I'm sure you'll both sleep abominably. As for you, Jane, don't fail to be on your veranda tomorrow to see me pass!"

He glanced into the street, at the stone parapet by the canal, the bollards between the trees, the shaped gables of the houses opposite. When he shut the door, he stood still for a moment, his hand to his heart, since once again he had that sudden feeling of constriction that had caused him so much alarm. For a second he thought of calling one of his colleagues, a heart specialist who had seen him previously and had told him it was nothing to worry about.

It seemed to him strange for some reason to be alone in the empty hall, standing under the light, which was in the form of a lantern with colored glass sides. At the far end was the kitchen door, whose frosted-glass panels were lit up. Now and again a shadow moved across them.

Upstairs all was darkness. Here, the umbrella stand, which also had its history. Another little quarrel. Alice had given it to him for his birthday, and his idea of a birthday present was something for your own personal use. So annoyed had he been that he had threatened to give her a box of cigars for hers.

How silly it all was! And how far, far away! Like the coatstand. Alice had wanted one of fumed oak, he one of bamboo. There'd been an argument, Alice maintaining that bamboo was common.

They had bought one of fumed oak with bronze pegs and a bevel-edged looking-glass in the middle. They had bought it at Versma's, the best furniture store in Sneek.

Kuperus could follow the Van Malderens all the way home. Jane, as always hanging on her husband's arm, out of breath because he took such long strides. And it wasn't hard to guess that they'd be talking about him. . . .

And then their arrival home, to their newly built house, one of the smartest in town . . . Jane heaving a sigh of satisfaction as she took off her outdoor shoes, which cramped her feet.

Like a nightmare, the discomfort in his chest passed off. He crossed the hall and opened the kitchen door. The new maid, Beetje, was ironing, while Neel was cutting thin slices of cheese.

"When would you like dinner?" she asked.

"As soon as possible. You can set the table now."

He was tired all of a sudden. Was there a chance of their doing anything to him in the Billiard Club? Would they have the courage to replace him? It was an important question. It wasn't the billiards that counted, but the circle of people who made up the club. All the best people belonged, and there was nothing in Sneek that quite compared with it. Even the café itself was not like any other. If it wasn't exactly reserved for the notabilities of the town, few went there who did not come under that classification, and when they did, they were generally made to feel out of place.

If they asked him to resign, it could only mean that they suspected him. In fact, it would almost amount to a public accusation.

Rather than that, they had approached Franz Van Malderen. . . . Franz had spoken to his wife. . . . His wife had invited herself to tea. . . . And, after a little maneuvering, she had broached the subject of a trip abroad. And the young

126

widow! Of course, if he married abroad, there was all the less chance of his ever coming back.

When Neel came in with the tablecloth, he was still holding his wife's photograph. Suddenly conscious of it, he put it down quickly, but not before she had seen it.

"There are too many things in here," he said roughly. "We must get rid of some of these photographs."

To which Neel answered:

"It wouldn't be right."

For the life of her, she couldn't have given a reason. It was always like that with her. It just wasn't the thing to do. It wouldn't be right.

He shrugged his shoulders, then paused to study her. Jane had not failed to notice the change in her. Her hair was neatly done and her whole appearance showed signs of care. Kuperus even came to the conclusion she must be using face powder.

He had told the truth when he'd boasted of having her eat with him. It had started only a few days before.

"Why don't you sit down?" he had said as she stood waiting.

"I wouldn't like to."

"Why not?"

"It's not the right thing."

"Well, you're going to do it anyway!" he had

snapped. "From now on you're going to have your meals with me. Do you hear that?"

She had hardly been able to swallow a thing, but all the same she had had a meal with him, and with that a new custom had been inaugurated. As for Beetje, Kuperus didn't bother about what she might think. On the contrary, he positively flaunted his relationship with Neel, going into the kitchen at night on purpose to say:

"Coming to bed, Neel? Good night, Beetje."

Beetje didn't seem to understand. Or if she did, it was a matter of complete indifference to her. She worked twelve to fourteen hours a day, and to judge by the expression on her face — or the lack of it — she didn't have a thought in her head the whole day long.

"You can leave the wine here," he said.

Half the second bottle was left. And habit was so strong in him that he couldn't help getting out the special silver-mounted cork, which they had always used for bottles that had been opened. It was part of a plated service that had come from The Hague. They had chosen it from a catalogue, and within two years the plating had worn off.

"I'm tired, Neel," he sighed, sinking back into the chair in which Van Malderen had sat.

And when the meal was served he complained:

"I'm not hungry."

"You'd better eat something. . . . It's not good to go to bed on an empty stomach."

Exactly what his wife would have said, or Jane Van Malderen, or any other woman, for that matter.

"They came about the electricity," added Neel, "and I paid the bill."

And every object was in its exact place, immutably, unbearably in its place!

SIX

Still only half awake, Neel had not had time to light the kitchen fire and was warming up the coffee on a gas ring. Kuperus had shaved with cold water. He reached the kitchen at the same time at Beetje, who had obviously just been wrenched from her sleep, too.

"I'll have it here," he said.

He sat down at a corner of the table. Neel gave him his coffee, then stood dreamily watching him. It was six o'clock in the morning. It was March now, but it was still cold.

"Will you wear your fur coat?" she asked.

"I think I'd better."

The streets were deserted. Carrying a small suitcase, Kuperus walked briskly toward the station, accompanied only by the sound of his own steps. Not till he got near the station was he joined by others, obviously making for the same place.

Suddenly it occurred to him that this was the first time he'd taken the train since the event had happened. The month before, he hadn't even thought of the Biological Association, and apart from the monthly meetings he hardly ever went on a train.

The station was only just beginning to come to life. At the ticket office he had to knock on the shutter for it to be opened.

"Amsterdam. First class."

It was only as Kuperus was going, ticket in hand, toward the barrier that he realized that the collector might know something. Why hadn't he thought about it before? He held out his ticket and stared hard at the fair young man with bad teeth who punched it.

Would he have remembered that, on the night in question, Kuperus had not handed in his ticket, and had not even gotten off at Sneek?

Under the doctor's stare, a look of surprise came into the other's pale blue eyes and a line formed on his forehead, perhaps with the effort to remember. But there was nothing unusual in his voice as he said:

"Good morning, Doctor!"

It was a matter of a few seconds, not long enough to draw any conclusions. Yet the fact remained that the man had looked surprised and frowned slightly.

Kuperus took his usual seat in his usual carriage, where he was sure of being undisturbed.

As the train started off, a ray of sunshine lit up the sky just behind the sails of a windmill. It was exactly like a picture postcard or a holiday poster.

The doctor leaned forward to look at the man who had punched his ticket. The latter was standing on the platform looking back at him.

The important thing was to know what he would do, or whether he'd do anything. Would he remember not having seen Kuperus that night? If he was in doubt, he might even hunt through the used tickets. Surely they would be kept somewhere or other.

And then, would he go to the police? Kuperus had been seen getting into the train at Staveren, and the stationmasters would doubtless be able to say that he hadn't got off at Hindeloopen, Workum, or IJlst.

So everything depended on the chance ideas that might enter a certain railwayman's head. If he said anything, they'd know that Kuperus had got out of the train between stations. And if they knew that. . .

"Tell the boss to send me some dough. I mean it."
That had been the last sentence in Karl's letter to Neel. Nothing more. No particulars. No threats. Karl was down and out and asking for money: that was all. Kuperus had taken his

address, having decided to go and see him when he went to Amsterdam.

At eight o'clock they got to Staveren, where the boat was waiting alongside. The sun was already warm, and Kuperus regretted having worn his fur coat. The Zuider Zee was a pale silky blue, its rippled surface dotted with the sails of two or three dozen fishing boats.

Everything happened as usual. The train whistled, the ship's bell rang. The passengers made straight for the saloon, where they ordered tea. Kuperus went down with the others, but saw nobody he knew. He couldn't help feeling, however, that the steward looked at him in a rather peculiar way, so he changed his mind and went back on deck, where he sat with his suitcase beside him, staring first at the receding church spire of Staveren, then, a quarter of an hour later, at the town of Enkhuizen, lit up by the morning sun.

After all, the man at Sneek might only have been surprised by the way the doctor had looked at him. Or perhaps he'd simply been curious to see Kuperus after reading about the case in the papers.

Kuperus was not planning to go to his sister-in-law's. No, he was going to the Ritz. For years he'd looked in through the revolving doors of the hotel and longed to go in. But things were different now. In it was a world he had never dreamed of rubbing shoulders with, people whose luggage was plastered all over with the labels of grand hotels, and a bus belonging to one of the airlines was often drawn up outside.

Why shouldn't he go to the Ritz, too? What was there to stop him? For that matter, what was there to stop him from taking a plane to Paris, to London, to Berlin?...

He went as usual, however, to have his glass of gin in the bar opposite the station. It reminded him of the fatal day.

The Ritz was at the end of the street, near the shcp where he'd bought the revolver. He walked along in the sunshine, with the hundred and one noises of the town around him, threading his way through the busy crowd. And as he did so he wondered what he had been thinking about on that other morning.

He had walked along, just as he was doing now. But what had he been thinking about? Everything had been decided. He knew exactly what he was going to do. But why?

It was curious. He couldn't reconstitute the state of mind he'd been in that day.

He hadn't been particularly jealous. The fact of the matter was that, since the event, he had hardly so much as thought of Alice.

He was only about a hundred yards from the Ritz when a truth began to dawn upon him, a truth that made him go hot all over. He couldn't banish it. It stared him in the face. He hadn't really bought the revolver to kill his wife, but to kill...Schutter!

As for his reasons...No! It was better not to think about it at all. Better anything than that...

"A single room, please. A nice one."

"With bath?"

"Of course!"

"Here's one at ten guilders....Number 246..."

He was relieved of his suitcase, and found himself with nothing to do until two o'clock. In the lounge were some English people reading their newspapers. A young woman who looked like an actress was playing with a little dog with a squashed-in face.

Kuperus decided to go and see Karl.

Karl's street was narrow and dirty. And there weren't many streets in Amsterdam that could be called dirty. It had Chinese shops and shabby secondhand dealers. Some were not really shops at all. In spite of the few faded packs of cigarettes in the window, they plied a trade that was only too easy to guess, and two or three times Kuperus looked hastily away from eyes that were meant to be seductive.

When he got to Karl's number, he found it was a barber's. On the left was a low doorway leading to a dim staircase. On the second floor he found some children playing on the landing, who directed him to the floor above.

"Come in."

He pushed the door and found himself in a room where the remains of a meal littered the table. Karl was still in bed, and beside him a woman's hair straggled over the pillow.

"Oh, it's you!"

Karl sat up in bed, ran his hand over his face, yawned, then shook his companion.

"Come on! Get up! You can go for a little walk on the landing."

At that moment Kuperus almost envied him, almost envied him his sordid life and his in-difference to it. The girl got out of bed. She was slim and dark, with small pear-shaped breasts. She looked for her slippers, cast a mis-trustful glance at the visitor, threw a green coat over her nightgown, and went out. Karl didn't bother to get up; he merely sat on the edge of the bed. A shaft of sunshine fell on his bare legs.

"It's nice of you to bring the money. How's Neel?"

"Quite all right, thank you."

"I don't need a lot. Fifty guilders would keep me going for a while."

The young man scratched his head, then his feet. He seemed to find it difficult to wake up. The window was narrow. The girl's dress lay on the floor, and some not very clean underclothes.

Kuperus did not answer. He hesitated, embarrassed, while the other looked at him quizzically, ironically.

"You're a funny sort of fellow," he said at last.

"Why?" asked the doctor.

"No particular reason...Anyway, it's none of my business."

Did that mean that he knew? If he didn't know, would he have asked for the money with such assurance?

"I'd like to ask you a question," said Kuperus after another pause. "What was it made you leave Germany?"

"An accident...a silly accident...I'd discovered a little servant who had all her savings hidden in her room....And one day I thought I'd help myself to them. I felt sure she'd hold her tongue, but instead of that she started hollering for all she was worth. I just had time to throw her on her bed...."

Kuperus listened, trembling with eagerness.

"...and put a pillow over her face."

He got up with a scowl on his face, and looked for his toothbrush.

"I held it there till she quieted down, then bolted. . . . It was two days later that I saw in the papers that she was dead. . . . A pity! She was a nice girl. . . . Much the same as Neel — one of those who seem to agree with everything you say, but you can never tell what's going on in their heads. . . ."

The scowl on his face had deepened. He passed a wet towel roughly over his face and put on his trousers, then turned to Kuperus.

"What about you?" he asked casually.

"What do you mean?"

"What have you done?"

"Me?"

Karl shrugged his shoulders.

"Just as you like!" he said. "As I said before, it's none of my business. . . . Besides, these things are not so funny that you want to go on talking about them. . . . Did Neel send me any message?"

"No."

"I expect she'll write. . . . She looks as soft as they make 'em. . . . But I don't mind betting she'd holler, too, just like the other. . . ."

He opened the door. The girl was sitting in her green coat on the bottom step of the next flight.

"You can come in now," he said.

And to Kuperus:

"Now you know where I live. . . . I've taken this room by the month. . . . Any time, if I can be of any use to you. . . ."

And he held out a ten-guilder note to the girl saying:

"Get me some cigarettes."

Kuperus didn't want to go. Something held him back, some obscure need to see more of this man who had also killed someone.

"What's the matter?" asked Karl.

"Nothing."

"I daresay it's upset you a bit — what I've just said. . . . You needn't worry. That's the kind of thing one doesn't want to do twice. . . ."

And still Kuperus couldn't make up his mind to go.

"Is there anything you want to say to me?" asked Karl. "Don't forget I'm not pressing you to tell me anything. . . ."

"No! I'll go. . . ."

It was high time he did! In another minute he'd have blurted out everything to this man.

"So long, Doctor. . . If there's anything you can do for me, I'll let you know. . . . You can do the same."

It felt strange, a minute or two later, to find himself once again in a broad busy street on which ordinary people were coming and going on foot, on bicycles, in streetcars or private cars. A street of shop windows, some piled high with cakes and pastries, others with dummies dressed in ready-made clothes.

There was only one thing that came out quite clearly from the conversation, and that was that Karl had killed a servant accidentally, just to save himself from being caught.

And Kuperus? In the eyes of the world, his case would be clearer still. They'd put it down to jealousy without a second's hesitation. Jealousy! That, no doubt, was why they spoke of being sorry for him. Was it because they were sorry for him that they'd made him president of the club?

Anyhow, they were making a great mistake. Jealousy had nothing to do with it. Nor revenge either. He wasn't angry at Alice, and never had been. He'd practically forgotten all about her until the other day when he'd picked up her photograph. Since then he'd picked it up often and...yes, and even regarded it with a subtle contentment. Moreover, more than once he'd picked up the bit of blue knitting and played with it in his hand.

There'd been a row about that. Seeing the wool, Neel had wanted to put it away, or perhaps even throw it away, but to her great surprise the doctor had suddenly flared up.

"You leave that where it is, do you hear?...
I won't have you changing anything in the
room...."

Why should he bother about it?

As for Karl, he wasn't ready to let anything
get him down. He moved along in his filth and
squalor, always finding some woman or other
to wait on him, and, with a shrug of his shoulders, saying of his victim:

"A pity! She was a nice girl."

He didn't enjoy his lunch at all. That was a
pity, too, since it was the first time he'd had a
meal at the Ritz. There were a lot of people
there, which may have helped to make him feel
lonely, sitting at a table by himself. He opened
a newspaper, but couldn't concentrate on what
he was reading, and he scarcely knew what he
was eating.

At two o'clock he arrived at his meeting, and
he had no sooner set foot in the spacious hall,
with its Corinthian columns and huge blue and
white flagstones, than he regretted having come.

It was no more than an impression, but it was
enough to upset him. All his colleagues who
were waiting there seemed to have their backs
turned toward him or to be so deeply engaged
in conversation that they didn't notice him.

Of course they'd have real all about the affair in the papers, which had even published photographs of Kuperus himself. But was that sufficient reason?

He went up to one of them, whom he knew particularly well, and held out his hand. The other, who had been a student with him, took it rather awkwardly.

"Hello. How are you?"

"Pretty well, thanks," answered Kuperus.

"You're not looking any too good. You need a rest."

"Yes . . . As a matter of fact, I've only dropped in to make my excuses. I've got an appointment in an hour. . . ."

"Leave it to me. I'll tell the chairman you couldn't stay."

It was the first time Kuperus had beaten a retreat. But there had really been too many of them, and the atmosphere of the place was somewhat intimidating at the best of times. Besides, he was thinking all the time about Karl.

Hadn't that young man discovered the right way to live? He made no demands on life. He simply went his own way and did exactly what he liked.

As on that other afternoon, Kuperus went to the movie house. This time it was a musical comedy. All the characters, in elaborate costume, seemed to spend their whole lives singing and waltzing.

It was dark when he got out again, and the streets were crowded with people going home from work.

A happy throng! People rushing home hungry for their supper, after which they'd sleep like children.

What made him think suddenly of his first pocket knife? He had been eleven at the time. For months and months he had longed for a knife, but had never had enough money to buy one. Finally, he had sold two of his schoolbooks to a secondhand dealer and then pretended he'd lost them.

With the proceeds, he'd got the knife. Only, of course, it had to be kept secret. If anyone had seen it, questions would have been asked. So he could only use it when alone. At first he'd even locked himself in the lavatory just to take it out of his pocket and have a look at it.

There was no reason why he should think of it now. But neither was there any reason for anything else. No reason why he should be walking all alone through the streets of Amsterdam, no reason to spend the night at the Ritz, no reason to take the train next day and then the boat at Enkhuisen and then the train again.

Back in Sneek he would stare once more at the man who took tickets. And be no wiser than he was now.

Around him was a town, a country, a whole world. And in all that world there was just one little corner that was his. An easy chair by a big tiled stove with brass fittings, a glow of rose-colored light shining down on a dining-room table, a servant who didn't mind if she did. . . .

His practice had been dwindling day by day. One day he had sat for a whole hour in his office waiting for a patient to turn up.

Then why didn't they arrest him? If that's what they really thought, why didn't they come to the point?

He went back to the Ritz, but left again almost immediately. He started walking. It wasn't that he wanted to walk. To tell the truth, he didn't want to do anything. He had thought that the atmosphere of the big town would do him good. Instead, he was ill at ease there.

If there'd been a night train, he'd have taken it, and burst into the kitchen in the morning, surprising that little slut of a Beetje, and Neel, to whom he'd have given a pat on her behind.

Finding himself once again in front of the barber shop, he hesitated, then made up his mind and went upstairs and knocked on Karl's door. It was the one opposite that opened, and an old man said:

"You'll find him in the little bar five doors down the street."

Kuperus had never been in a bar of that kind before. It was a step down from street level, and was barely furnished with four tables and a bar. The smell of gin was nauseating. In a corner, two sailors were drinking in silence. As for Karl, he was sitting at a table by himself, swilling down a sausage with a glass of beer.

"You again?...Is anything wrong?"

"I was bored."

"That's easily cured. Here! A double gin!"

Kuperus gulped it down in one go, while Karl calmly went on eating.

"And what's boring you?"

"I don't know."

"Have another gin. I'll stand you this one."

He wiped his mouth, leaned back in his seat, and looked attentively at the doctor.

"Do you mind if I give you some advice?" he asked at last. "If you go on like this much longer, you'll come to a bad end...."

"So that's what you think, is it?"

"I don't think anything....Your affairs are no business of mine."

"Come on! Tell me what you really think."

Kuperus was simply dying to talk about it. His tone was one of supplication. He had to talk. He couldn't go on bottling it up indefinitely.

"Why should I think anything?"

"You know perfectly well."

Karl had made a sign to the effect that the man behind the bar was listening to them. He tapped on the marble table with a coin and paid for the drinks.

"Let's go."

They went along a street where somebody was playing an accordion, and nearly bumped into a drunk. Women were loitering on the sidewalk, but there was no need for Karl to brush them aside; they made way for him themselves.

At the end of the street, they came to a canal. The quays were deserted and the only signs of life came from three lighted barges moored alongside each other. Kuperus had a burning feeling in his chest from the gin he had drunk, which had really been some crude and fiery spirit.

"Now what is it you have to tell me?"

"Do you sometimes think of — you know what I mean — that servant you...?"

Karl looked into his eyes, as far as the darkness allowed him to.

"What of it?"

"That's all!"

146

"Go on! You might just as well cough it up. Do you think I can't see you've got something on your mind?"

It was too late to turn back, but Kuperus was suddenly frightened just the same. He wondered what on earth had prompted him to open the subject.

Wasn't he putting himself at the mercy of this German? The latter knew he had money on him and could with the greatest of ease push him into the canal. Only, why do a thing like that, when blackmail was so much safer?

"You know the truth, don't you?" stammered the doctor.

"So it was you, was it?"

It was said without a trace of surprise.

"I might have known it from the moment you called Neel into your room. . . . It always has that effect on a man. . . ."

"I don't understand."

"Never mind. It doesn't matter. . . . Now tell me what you want with me."

"Nothing."

Karl shrugged his shoulders in the darkness, then lit a cigarette. He hesitated a moment, wondering whether to go or stay. When at last he spoke, it was to say:

"I may as well tell you just what I think: the

147

trouble with you is you've got some vicious kink in you!"

Some vicious kink in him!

He was on the boat. And once more he had succeeded in making everybody feel uncomfortable. This time he was traveling on a Wednesday — in other words, with the mayors of Staveren, Leeuwarden, and Sneek, with whom he had always played bridge during the crossing.

Kuperus knew perfectly well that they didn't want to play with him, or even be seen in his company. But he also knew they'd find it very difficult to refuse. And when they got down to the saloon, they found him already installed at their usual table, shuffling a pack of cards.

What could they do but accept the situation? Even the steward was embarrassed. When the mayor of Staveren came to deal, he misdealt twice in a row. Each of them avoided saying anything except what was strictly necessary to the game.

A vicious kink! Did he really have something of the kind? Was he perhaps a pathological case? He played his hands, but all the time thought of other things, too. He thought of Karl, of Neel, and of Beetje bringing their coffee to them in bed in the mornings. He had insisted on her doing that.

For a while his mind wandered; then suddenly his thoughts were narrowed down to one – that everyone suspected him. No. It was more than that. Everyone was *convinced* he was the murderer. But they didn't arrest him! They didn't even question him! Perhaps they were waiting for some proof, like the ticket he hadn't handed in. Perhaps they really were sorry for him and were ready to shut their eyes. Or it might have been merely to avoid a scandal.

That was more likely. To avoid a scandal. The Van Malderens had tried to persuade him to go away so that the whole affair could be hushed up and forgotten.

But he hadn't fallen in with their little plan. On the contrary, by staying in Sneek he was forcing them every day to shake hands with a murderer. What did they think about *that*? Were they scared of him?

In any case, he wasn't going away. If he'd ever thought of it, this journey to Amsterdam would have been enough to choke off the idea. He simply couldn't face the thought of living anywhere else but in Sneek, in his own house, his own familiar little corner. He was longing to be back there among the familiar objects that had surrounded him for so many years.

"Three no trump."

The mayor of Staveren went up on deck a few minutes before they arrived, and was the first down the gangway, so as not to be seen landing with Kuperus. As usual, the latter had his first-class compartment to himself.

It was dark, too, just as it had been two months before.

"Hindeloopen!"

And ten minutes later:

"Workum!"

Then:

"IJlst!"

Suddenly he went pale, because the train slowed down just as it had the other time. Perhaps it was the usual thing, only he'd never noticed it before. He got up from his seat and had his hand on the door handle.

But it didn't stop after all, and a few minutes later he was handing in his ticket at Sneek. He looked into the man's eyes, and the man looked into his as he said:

"Thank you, Doctor."

Had he always said thank you like that? He couldn't remember, and he wondered whether the words contained a threat.

He walked into the center of town with his suitcase in his hand, and paused outside the lighted windows of the Onder den Linden.

It was the one thing left to do to finish up

the day., To go inside and oblige them all to shake hands with him, to sit among them and stare at them defiantly!

Van Malderen was there. He seemed embarrassed.

"Been to Amsterdam?"

"Yes."

Billiard balls rolled across the brightly lighted tables. In a corner, four members of the club were playing bridge.

Van Malderen's question, asked merely for form's sake, and the half-hearted handshakes of the others – that was all he had of human contact with these people. Even Old Willem wasn't the same as before. When he brought him his glass of beer, he seemed to do so with some mental reservation.

To annoy them, Kuperus asked:

"What's become of that charming girl? . . . What was her name? Oh, yes! Lina!"

He looked insistently at Loos, then at Van Malderen. Some of the others looked embarrassed or smirked.

"She's gone."

"Really? What, all alone?"

"No. With that Englishman who was here."

An Englishman had been staying in town, to study the manufacture of Dutch cheese. At one of the tables Kuperus saw his friend the examining magistrate. He nodded to him but got no response. Perhaps the other hadn't noticed.

It was as though there was a vacuum around him, a hollow emptiness in which the clack of the billiard balls echoed strangely and in which an occasional voice struck a false note. If he left, it would have been a relief to everybody, he knew very well, and for that very reason he made a point of staying, ordering another glass of beer and then a gin.

The gin reminded him of the previous evening, when he'd had a lot of it, so much that by the time he'd got back to the Ritz he'd been pretty thoroughly drunk, and he really couldn't remember how he'd got to bed. He had awakened in a state of anxiety, expecting Karl to turn up at any moment with demands for money, backed by threats. Nobody had appeared, however, and he'd caught his usual train.

"How's Jane?" he asked Van Malderen.

"Very well, thanks..."

Everyone was against him. Every way he turned, he came up against a blank wall. And in addition to all the people who suspected him, there was one who knew. For Kuperus was not forgetting the anonymous letter.

"An accident," Karl had said, speaking of the girl he'd suffocated with a pillow.

152

But there wasn't anything accidental about the shooting of Schutter and Alice, was there? Unless a kink could be called an accident! Could it?

What had made Karl say that about a vicious kink?

Vicious indeed! A man who'd lived forty-five years of unblemished respectability? He had never deceived his wife, except once, in Paris, and that had been a silly little affair of no importance. Even so, it had given him weeks of nightmares, because he was afraid he might have picked up some disease. The pocket knife had been dishonest, admittedly, but that could be dismissed as a misdeed of childhood.

Vicious indeed! To live fifteen years in the same house, and buy his wife new furniture when it wasn't necessary at all? To go every evening to the Billiard Club, and have as his one and only ambition to become its president?

Vicious indeed! To get out of bed at night ten or twenty times a month to deliver babies?

It was enough to make one weep!

"A gin, Willem . . ."

Never mind if it was one too many. Never mind if the others looked at him reprovingly. He needed to know, and the gin helped him in the job of self-examination.

In Karl's case, there was no room for doubt.

He had suffocated a girl accidentally, his intention being merely to stop her screaming.

But he? Why had he done what he had?... That still had to be found out.

His head was heavy as he stood up.

"Who'd like two hundred up with me?" he asked.

No one answered. His cheeks were flushed, and his eyes were glassy as he glared at them one after the other.

"I asked who'd like a game with me?" he insisted.

He could feel the gin mounting to his head, but imagined the others couldn't see it. It was Franz Van Malderen who, as his oldest friend, finally took it upon himself to answer:

"Why don't you go home to bed?"

And just as he could hardly remember undressing the night before in Amsterdam, he had, next morning, only the vaguest idea of how he'd left the café, where his departure had been followed by a long silence, then by a sudden burst of conversation.

SEVEN

It was ten o'clock in the morning, and Kuperus had not yet finished dressing. Standing in front of the mirror, he was in the act of tying his tie when all at once he paused, motionless, listening.

Through the wall came the sound of a piano, at first a few casual notes, then some firmer chords, which formed the opening bars of one of Schumann's compositions.

For a moment he was at a loss to know what it was that had caught him off guard. It wasn't surprise, but, rather, some sort of wistful nostalgia. As he looked at his reflection, he saw a Kuperus different from that of the last few days, a Kuperus who was touched, agitated, bewildered.

"Mia!" he whispered.

Mia had returned. Perhaps she was cured. The doctor was so affected by the idea that he almost forgot he had been summoned to appear before the examining magistrate.

The house next door, on the side toward the bridge, was smaller than the others, but it was more spick-and-span than any of them, with its woodwork freshly painted every year and its white curtains starched. In it lived the Braundts, the quietest and most respected people on the street. Braundt was a master at the grammar school; his wife was housekeeper in an upper school for girls.

They went off at the same time every day, leaving their little girl, Mia, in the care of a governess. Mia was twelve. She didn't go to school because of her health and also because she spent a lot of time studying the piano. For the last two years, Kuperus had been used to hearing her practice while he saw his patients.

The autumn before, she had been so ill that they'd sent her off to spend the winter in Switzerland, and the doctor had so far forgotten her that he had ceased to notice the absence of the music.

And now she had come back, and the sound of her playing filled his house.

"The little girl's come back," said a voice behind him.

It was Neel, who was busily brushing his bowler.

"Yes, she's back," he murmured.

Downstairs, he didn't go out at once, but

wandered first into the living room. Against the wall was an upright piano, the top of which was littered with photographs and ornaments.

On the music stool was a cushion of dark crimson plush, which had been made specially for little Mia.

At one time, she had come in regularly every afternoon to do her practicing under the supervision of Madame Kuperus. For Alice played, too, though not well enough to give the child her lessons. For that, a teacher came to the Braundts' every morning.

Alice had kept a special box of chocolates for Mia. Perhaps it was still there in the dining-room sideboard.

"Will you be seeing any patients while you're out? If so, you'd better take your bag."

Neel followed him to the front door.

"No. I won't need it."

He had been quite relieved, that morning, to receive the official notice asking him to be at the examining magistrate's office by eleven o'clock. Somehow, its effect had been to set his mind at rest. But Mia's playing had sufficed to upset him again, and it was with a heavy heart that he heard the familiar sound of the front door shutting behind him.

Many a time Mia had still been with Alice when her mother had come back from work in the evening. If so, the latter had simply banged on the wall, which was the signal for the child to return home.

It was a dull gray day. Kuperus made an effort to shake off the melancholy effect of the music. He succeeded sufficiently to be able to throw a glance of complete indifference at the veranda from which he knew Jane Van Malderen would be watching him. In fact, he was almost tempted to put out his tongue!

What was the examining magistrate going to call him? Anton Groven and Hans Kuperus had been to school together, and by rights should call each other by their Christian names. They always had. It's true they had never seen a great deal of each other, but that was only because his wife was the most disagreeable woman in Sneek. Nobody could stand her.

Why had he been summoned? Had the writer of the anonymous letter come forward at last? Or had the ticket collector been to the police?

When he'd got up that morning, Kuperus had been in a pugnacious mood, ready to confront the world and answer whatever questions they cared to put to him. But a few notes of music had cut the ground from under his feet, bringing back the past, years and years of it, right from the time of Mia's first scales, when she'd had to have two cushions on the music stool.

The law courts were grayer than the rest of the town. The doctor walked straight upstairs and knocked on the examining magistrate's door. Before there was any answer, he heard the sound of chairs being moved inside.

Finally the door was opened by the magistrate's clerk. Anton Groven stood rather uneasily behind his desk, trying to look dignified.

"Come in... Take a seat..."

He didn't shake hands. He didn't call his visitor by his Christian name. Sitting down again, he tugged at his little beard, while with the other hand he turned over the papers of a file whose bulk surprised Kuperus.

"I had to summon you to come. There are a few questions I must ask you before winding up this inquiry. I've received reports from various quarters, and there are one or two points that require elucidation...."

He had obviously rehearsed the sentences beforehand, since he sounded rather like a schoolboy reciting one of the fables of La Fontaine. He hadn't even raised his eyes from the dossier.

"For instance, I see here that at the time of the incident you were sheltering a certain Karl Vorberg, of German nationality, whose record is highly unsatisfactory. The Emden police have informed us that this Vorberg is strongly suspected of having committed a murder, but there's not sufficient evidence to provide grounds for extradition. . . ."

At last Groven raised his head. He looked timidly at Kuperus, as though he feared the latter would present a painful spectacle.

"Were you aware of the presence of this Vorberg in your house?"

"No."

"In that case, I'm afraid I must quote from another report. It states here that you saw this person twice yesterday in a street of ill repute in Amsterdam. Do you deny that?"

"No."

Kuperus tried to banish the strains of the piano from his mind. He realized now that, though he had been left alone, he had none-theless been the subject of pretty exhaustive inquiries. He had even been followed. And he hadn't noticed it!

He looked at the dossier. Was every page of it a trap in some form or other?

"Don't think I'm trying to trip you up. . . . But we must get this clear. . . . On the one hand, you've told me you didn't know Vorberg. On the other, you admit having seen him twice yesterday. . . ."

160

"That's right."

"Would you mind explaining that, please?"

"I didn't know Karl at the time. I had no idea there was a man sleeping in the house. . . ."

"How did you find out?"

"From the maid. When I took her as my mistress."

The clerk hesitated to write that down, and Groven looked inquiringly at the doctor, who went on:

"I take full responsibility for what I'm saying. I had the maid down to sleep with me, and then it came out that she had another man upstairs. . . . To get rid of him, I gave him some money, on condition he go to Amsterdam."

"Has he been blackmailing you?"

"No. But it's only natural he should expect a little compensation for obliging me. Yesterday I gave him a little more to get along with."

For a moment there was silence while Groven studied his papers. Then he looked up again and made a sign to the clerk not to take down what he was going to say.

"The presence of this German under your roof was the most obscure part of the whole affair, and the police were almost prepared to draw certain conclusions from it. . . . It will be easy to have your story confirmed by the servant and by Karl Vorberg himself. . . . With that out

161

of the way, there's not much to bother about...."

That might have been taken ironically, since there were at least a hundred typewritten sheets in the dossier, and presumably they weren't about nothing!

"I suppose," went on the magistrate, "that, on your side, you've no information to give us...."

He said that rather hurriedly, as though he was afraid the doctor might have.

"I'm ready to answer your questions," answered the latter.

"I wish I could spare myself the task of having to ask them.... As you know, of course, Schutter's wallet disappeared, which suggested an obvious motive. But we couldn't blind ourselves to the fact that there might be another one — in other words, jealousy. I take it that you deny having shot your wife and her companion...."

Kuperus sat still for a moment, assailed by a strange temptation. He would have loved to contradict the magistrate. He would have loved to answer:

"I don't deny any such thing!"

But it wasn't so easy. And if, in the end, he nodded, it was because Groven, by the attitude he adopted, practically forced him to.

"That evening, when you returned from

162

Amsterdam, you went as usual to the Onder den Linden, after which you went straight home."

Groven breathed deeply. He was relieved. He made a little movement of his hand as though to banish the clouds.

"Of course, if it was assumed to be a crime of passion, the sentence would be correspondingly lenient, as it always is in such cases....On the other hand, it would unloose a scandal that could only be described as disastrous...."

Kuperus gave a bleak smile.

"On your side, is there anybody on whom you could throw suspicion?"

"No. Nobody," answered Kuperus without a trace of sarcasm.

The magistrate paused while the clerk wrote that down. Then he stood up and cleared his throat. He had come to the most difficult part of all, but he was determined to go through with it.

"I hope," he began, looking everywhere but at Kuperus, "I hope you fully realize the situation. This crime, this double crime, was committed in such a way as to leave us with no serious indications as to the perpetrator, or, at all events, with no formal proof. If the case was sent before the Assizes, it's more than probable there'd be an acquittal, because the accused would be given the benefit of the doubt...."

The clerk had got up, too, and had disappeared into an alcove, where he was washing his hands.

"The accused?" asked Kuperus. "Who do you mean?"

"I don't know.... I'm just speaking in the abstract.... But let me go on. At this stage we can hardly hope for any fresh evidence. That's why I've asked you to come today. By this evening there's every probability that the case will have been dropped.... And, if it's dropped, the important thing is that it should be forgotten; in other words, there should be nothing to keep it fresh in people's minds.... You understand me, Doctor?"

He'd said "Dcotor"! That made it thoroughly official! Admittedly, it would have been difficult for Groven to call him Hans.

"As a matter of fact, one of our mutual friends, Van Malderen to be exact, told me you were intending to go away as soon as the case was finished.... And I must say I think it's a very wise decision...."

He had come out with it at last! With his hands in his pockets, he walked slowly to and fro behind his desk, pronouncing his words syllable by syllable to give full weight to all they were meant to convey.

164

"Your answers to my questions have been entirely satisfactory, and I feel sure that, before the day is out, what you have told me will be confirmed from other sources. That leaves us with only one or two details that are a little troublesome, though I don't suppose they would amount to much in the eyes of a jury. At the station they've hunted for your railway ticket without success. The man at the barrier has admitted that some people, particularly the regular passengers, occasionally leave the station via the buffet, in which case they don't hand in their tickets. . . . You can imagine what capital a lawyer could make out of an admission like that!"

There was no doubt about it: his words were intended as a threat. He spoke in tones of the utmost detachment, but he was nonetheless giving orders.

"And, last, the other little point: it's a pity that on the day in question you failed to attend the meeting of the Biological Association. Of course I'm quite sure you had a very good reason. I daresay you weren't feeling well that day and decided to come straight home. . . . And we mustn't forget that you've never possessed a revolver, and the one with which the crime was committed has not been found. . . . So, all things considered. . . But I don't want to make a long story of it. All I wanted to do was to put my cards frankly on the table. . . . As I said before, by tonight this dossier will have been stuffed away in a pigeonhole, and tomorrow I'll be busy on something else. . . . It only remains for me to wish you an interesting journey and to express the hope that this unfortunate business will soon cease to trouble people's minds. . . . "

He stood still and looked Kuperus squarely and coldly in the face.

"I take it you have nothing to add?" he said sternly.

The doctor hesitated. Why should a phrase of the music once more run through his head? Finally, and with an abject air, he stammered:

"Nothing."

"In that case, we can consider it all over. Thank you."

He opened the door himself, keeping his right hand on the handle so that it wouldn't be available for shaking hands. His only farewell was a stiff bow, and the doctor left ignominiously, bumped into somebody in the hall, muttered an apology, and found himself in the street without knowing how he'd left the building.

So acutely was he suffering that he had to stop in the middle of the sidewalk outside a house and stand there with his hand over his heart. It wasn't merely a physical suffering. It affected mind and body alike. It was an utter prostration of his whole being.

But through his agony came a ray of light. The day before, he had still been wondering why he'd killed. Now he knew it. It was because of just what he was suffering now!

He had just been through the most abject humiliation of his whole life. A man who had been to school with him, and ever since had called him by his Christian name, had rapped him over the knuckles and practically ordered him out of the town.

It was impossible to interpret what he had said in any other way. He had told Kuperus he was no longer wanted in Sneek. He had told him to pack his bags and clear out!

What was humiliation? The feeling of impotence in the face of one's fellow creature, of inferiority that has to be openly admitted, the obligation to bend before another's will. . . .

And wasn't that just what he'd felt over and over again in his relations with Schutter? And when he had received the anonymous letter . . .

. . . Schutter, who was richer than he was, who had kept his youthful figure, who was a polished man of the world, who could do anything he liked, and get away with it! . . .

He was walking along the canal now, but

with unseeing eyes. When he got home, he walked straight past Neel in the hall without so much as a glance at her, and, taking refuge in his office, he shut and locked the door.

There he paced up and down, clenching his fists because of the music. It wasn't Schumann now, but a Chopin berceuse, whose romanticism he found absolutely unbearable. He felt like breaking down altogether, bursting into tears.

Anton Groven was no doubt saying to Van Malderen:

"It's all arranged. . . . He's going!"

And when Van Malderen went home to lunch, he'd say to Jane:

"It's all arranged. . . . He's going!"

And so from mouth to mouth. Later on, in the Onder den Linden, the billiard players would say between their breaks:

"Have you heard? . . . It's all arranged. . . . He's going!"

It was a sort of bloodless execution. And the Braundts would soon be saying to the little wide-eyed Mia:

"Aunt Kuperus is dead and Uncle Kuperus has gone away."

For Mia had been in and out of their house so much that she had been taught to call them Aunt and Uncle Kuperus.

And now, after all, it was in a sense Schutter who triumphed. He had always put Kuperus in the shade, and now he was actually banishing him!

Up and down he went, to and fro, not knowing what he was doing. Sometimes he stopped to fiddle with something on his desk.

He had been completely incapable of standing up for himself. He had left the examining magistrate's office like a beggar who has been refused alms! Had Anton Groven been watching him as he groped his way blindly along the hall? Had he felt a spark of pity at the sight of his drooping shoulders?

If only he could have wept! Tears might have brought some relief. The music jarred on his nerves to such an extent that he suddenly walked swiftly over to the wall and banged on it. But Mia didn't understand what he meant.

He had killed because...

It wasn't really clear even now. At least, it was the sort of revelation that cannot be expressed in words or fitted into any logical sequence of ideas.

It was something like this: for fifteen years he, Dr. Kuperus, had lived in this house with his wife.... He worked hard.... In the course of the morning he saw about twenty patients, and, because they were mostly poor people, the waiting room always smelled a bit. . . .

In the afternoon he went all over the town on foot, into stuffy rooms whose air was already heavy with impending death, and then at five o'clock he would reach the Onder den Linden, often only to be called away again before he'd finished a game. . . .

In the evening he read the newspaper while his wife did some needlework or knitting. Once a month the Van Malderens stayed to dinner, and once a month he went to Amsterdam, where his sister-in-law put him up for the night. . . .

He had been on a cruise to Spitzbergen and had had a holiday in Paris. . . .

For fifteen years things had gone on like that, because that was how they had to be. He'd been quite a stickler in his way. Everything had to be in its right place, everything done at the right time.

When his wife had wanted her living room refurnished, he'd agreed because Jane Van Malderen's had been refurnished the year before. When she had wanted a fur coat, he had thought it over for a month, which only reasonable and proper, and then had bought it for her birthday.

Only, from time to time something gnawed at him, from time to time he was assailed by a longing to break out of this harmonious exist-ence, to knock down this scaffolding of respect-ability. Such ideas, however, were no sooner entertained than they were brushed aside. That he was living his life in the right sort of way was obvious, since everybody else did precisely likewise. . . .

If he was occasionally tempted to make a pass at Neel, he immediately reproved himself, and was even ready to judge himself very severely. . . .

Then all of a sudden his wife. . . and Schut-ter!. . .

If it had been anyone else, it would have been different. But it had to be Schutter! The one man in Sneek who did *not* live like Dr. Kuperus and all the others. The one man who lived just as he wanted to, indulging every whim. And far from being punished for it, he was rewarded. He was made president of the Billiard Club! And no woman seemed able to withhold her favors from him.

Not even Alice Kuperus!. . .

What did it all amount to? That Kuperus was wrong. That he'd been wrong all his life. That he'd been led up the garden path – the straight and narrow path, into the bargain – and been led nowhere.

In other words, everything was false, rotten to the core, the house and everything in it, the new living-room furniture, the fur coat, the piano, and the crimson cushion that had been made for Mia...

There! That was why he'd killed! Because he was fed up with the whole bag of tricks, because things that for years had seemed right and proper, if not scared, now seemed idiotic, like the bottle of Burgundy that was brought up from the cellar religiously every Thursday and set by the side of the fire to take the chill off...

Because everything had been knocked sideways. Because he could no longer even listen to Mia's playing...

He had been taken in. That was it: taken in! He'd been a fool to believe in it all, to toe the line, all for nothing.... They had never even thought of making him vice-president of the club!

So why not get rid of this Schutter, and his wife into the bargain?

Having done that, he would kill himself, too. Or he could just give himself up and then have the satisfaction of telling them all exactly what he thought of them.

Things had worked out differently. Why? He really couldn't say. He hadn't killed himself. Nor had he given himself up. The only thing he had done to mark his protest was to take

Neel to bed with him.

And where did he stand now? He didn't know that either. He was crushed. He didn't even have the courage to look at himself in the mirror. Stamped on his retina was the vision of Anton opening the door and showing him out, bowing frigidly....

The music never stopped. Mia practiced six hours a day, because she was intending to become a virtuoso.

If only he could have wept! But no! He even screwed his face into a grimace, hoping to start it that way, but no sob came.

Opening the door he angrily shouted:

"Neel!"

Then, since she didn't come immediately, he went downstairs and found her setting the table in the dining room.

"Neel!"

She turned and looked at him apathetically.

"Tell me, Neel...are there any rumors going around in the neighborhood?"

"What do you mean?"

"The people that gossip in the shops, for instance – have they been saying anything new these last few days?"

"About you?"

"Yes, of course – about me."

"They say you're going away."

"Do they give any reason?"

Neel sighed.

"You know perfectly well."

"Never mind! I want you to tell me."

"Oh, very well! They say that after what's happened you can't go on living in Sneek, and that even if you wanted to, you'd be prevented. . . ."

"Who says that?"

"Everybody. Even the boys run after me and put their tongues out. . . . You asked me to tell you, didn't you?"

"Do they say anything else?"

"They do."

"Come on! Out with it!"

"They say that you're much too cunning to have left any clues, but that the murderer of Schutter and your wife is not far away. . . ."

Kuperus looked at her out of the corner of his eye.

"And you?"

"What about me?"

"What do you think?"

"You know."

"Why should I?"

"Really? . . . Do you mean to say you don't know . . . that you never suspected?"

Her surprise was not put on.

"Suppose we drop the subject," she muttered,

moving toward the door.

"Answer me, will you?...What do you think?"

"I've known all along," she replied with a shrug of the shoulders. "You see, it was me who wrote the letter...."

She didn't seem to think it was of any importance. The subject bored her, and her one thought was to cut the conversation short.

"Why did you write that letter?"

"Because of Madame."

"Why?"

"I knew she came in late the nights you were in Amsterdam, and once she only got back at nine next morning...."

"Go on."

"One day we had a fight...."

"You and my wife?"

"Yes...I'd been doing the shopping, and was half a guilder short when I gave her the change....I must have dropped it somewhere, because I'd never think of taking the trouble to steal half a guilder....A whole hour she spent in the kitchen yelling at me and saying she'd take it out of my wages....It was then that I told her..."

"What did you tell her?"

"That if she did, I'd come out with what I knew."

Kuperus stood motionless, oppressed by the

thought of the petty squabbles that had gone on around him to which he'd been utterly oblivious. His life had been so quiet, so well regulated. He must have come home from the Onder den Linden only a few minutes after scenes of this kind, and had noticed nothing.

"But she was in such a temper that she yelled back at me: 'You'd never dare!' "

"But you did?"

"The same day . . . The next day she said she was sorry, gave me five guilders, and begged me to keep my mouth shut. . . . But it was too late. . . ."

"Did you tell her so?"

"No."

"And you took the five guilders?"

"Yes."

And from that day she had waited, surprised at having to wait so long. Because she knew that he knew.

"Did you ever ask her for money after that?"

"Toward the end, yes. On account of Karl."

She had made her confession without shame, only with a touch of asperity, as though she couldn't understand why anyone would want to stir up memories of that kind.

"So when I came back that night and told you to bring me some tea, you knew at once?"

"I knew from the moment you touched me."

The doctor was silent for a moment. Then he suddenly flared up.

"Get out of here!" he shouted. "Get out of this room."

In the mirror, he watched her go out shrugging her shoulders, then he went over and shut the door behind her. Coming back to the table, he caught hold of the tablecloth and, with a sudden jerk, sent all the china crashing to the floor. Finally he picked up a vase from the mantelpiece and hurled it, too, to the floor. It was a vase he had once mended himself, when a former servant, long before Neel, had broken off one of the handles.

There was no relief for his suffering! He was humiliated, humiliated by everything. Humiliated by Van Malderen, humiliated by Anton Groven, who was no doubt at that very moment discussing him with his wife as they sat at lunch...Humiliated by Neel...

Alice had paid the five guilders, hoping thus to buy Neel's silence....

A sudden stab went through him at a thought. It wasn't Alice who kept the housekeeping accounts, but he. So to give Neel five guilders, she must have cheated on the weekly bills. Or else...or else asked Schutter for it.

That was it! Surely! She'd asked Schutter. She'd sobbed out the whole story to him, and he'd reassured her, patted her on the back, given her the five guilders.

He looked around for something else to smash. But no! What was the use? It didn't even relieve his feelings. He was aching all over. He felt as though he were suffocating. He didn't know what to do with himself. The constriction in his chest got tighter and tighter, until it became sharp as a spasm. He groped for the handle of the door. He called out:

"Neel!"

She came, quite casually, asking:

"What is it now?"

"Call Dr. De Greef," he panted. "Ask him to come at once."

He felt sure his strength was failing. He thought the spasms of his heart were squeezing it like a sponge. He listened and heard Neel in the office talking to De Greef's maid. A moment later she came down again.

"He'll be here in a few minutes. Do you want anything else?"

"No. Leave me."

"You'd much better put it out of your mind. You won't do any good by worrying over it. . . . What's done's done. . . . "

"Be quiet."

"And what's the matter with a bit of foreign travel, anyway?"

"Hold your tongue, will you?"

He couldn't bear to listen to another word.

"Go away. Leave me alone."

Perhaps he was going to die. The music, which had stopped for a few minutes, now started again. He knew every note by now, every chord. He waited for each one to come. . . .

He left the door open, in order to be sure of hearing the bell when De Greef arrived.

EIGHT

Once again he groped for the switch and turned on the light. The hands of his watch were at half past eleven. For the fifth time he drank a glass of water, after which he lay down again and listened resentfully to the rain pattering on the roof.

It was very hot in the room, and his skin was tingling uncomfortably. If he turned over on his left side, he could feel a slight pain in his chest, but he knew now that it was nothing to worry about.

De Greef had said so, and he was a specialist of some standing whose reputation extended to Groningen and even to Amsterdam. But although he had been reassuring, that didn't mean he had been agreeable. On the contrary. When he came in, he had avoided offering Kuperus his hand.

"It's for you, is it?" he had grunted, taking off his gloves and putting his stethoscope down on the table.

180

A chilly little man, with gray hair and very white skin. His features were finely drawn, even sharp.

"Take your clothes off."

He was certainly thinking of other things than purely professional matters. And when Neel came in with a clean towel, he looked sideways at her. No doubt he had heard something about her, too.

"A feeling of suffocation, you say?"

"A spasm..."

"Take a deep breath."

He examined him standing. Kuperus looked enormous; in fact, De Greef's head came only to the level of his bare chest. For a quarter of an hour the examination went on, during which time the specialist asked a few curt questions, but made no comment whatsoever.

Finally, he called Neel and asked for some water to wash his hands. Then he started rolling up his shirt sleeves.

"Well?" asked Kuperus with some impatience.

"You're more frightened than anything else."

De Greef said it contemptuously, his voice as cold as his appearance.

"When one's as little ill as you are, there's no need to call in a specialist who's got plenty of serious work on his hands."

"Then I haven't got angina pectoris?"

"Not a shadow of it."

"But those spasms?"

The other shrugged his shoulders.

"Look here!" he said at last. "This isn't a job for a doctor at all. Speaking as a man, however, I can give you a bit of advice. Clear out! And as soon as possible. Take your servant with you if you can't do without her."

He had no sooner gone than the piano started up again, throwing Kuperus this time into a rage. He called Neel.

"Go next door and tell them to stop that damned piano!... Tell them I'm ill. Do you hear me?"

Neel heard him all right, but she shook her head.

"What are you waiting for?"

"I can't do that."

"What? Do you mean to say you refuse?"

"You know very well it isn't possible."

He really lost control, and all the more readily because he now knew it wasn't dangerous. He didn't have angina pectoris, not a shadow of it.

Cursing and swearing, he strode into the kitchen, where Beetje was washing up.

"Here! I want you.... Wipe your hands and go next door. Ask them, from Dr. Kuperus, to stop the piano for today...."

The girl looked inquiringly at Neel, who

182

shook her head. Thus prompted, she stammered:

"I can't."

"What did you say?"

"I can't."

It was a disgusting scene, sordid beyond words. He began by shaking the girl, who immediately burst into tears. Then, to stop her crying, he started slapping her face. At the same time, he stormed and threatened, heaping on Neel's head all the abuse he could think of.

Finally, panting with rage, he had left them and shut himself up in the dining room, where he found a bottle of gin in the sideboard, which he settled down to drink, muttering to himself all the while.

He hadn't had any dinner. He hadn't answered when Neel knocked on the door to come in and set the table. A little later he had gone up to the office, then to his bedroom, where he had started packing.

Now, he felt washed out. The sounds in the street had died down little by little, and the house, too, had relapsed into silence. There was nothing to be heard but the raindrops obstinately pattering down on the roof and against the windowpanes. The radiator seemed to be throwing out waves of heat.

Kuperus got up and slipped on his dressing gown. Opening the door, he went upstairs to the next floor, which was the attic. He moved noiselessly. Anyone seeing him might have thought he was afraid of himself.

Neel's door wasn't locked. He opened it and heard a rustling sound, as of someone roused from sleep. When he switched on the light, he found Neel's eyes open, looking at him.

The light made them blink, but they expressed nothing, neither surprise nor fear.

"What's the matter?"

She was hot, too. The whole house was overheated. There were two beds in the room; the other one was empty.

"Where's Beetje?"

"She's gone."

"What do you mean?"

"She's gone back to her parents."

"Because I slapped her?"

Neel's skin was shining; her eyelids were heavy.

"She wanted to go yesterday."

"Why?"

Neel sighed, as much as to say:

"You know as well as I do."

Kuperus looked fleetingly at her and said:

"Come downstairs."

"Oh, dear! Do you really want me to?"

"Yes. Do what I tell you."

She could see he was on the verge of losing his temper again, and grudgingly lifted herself up, thrust one leg out of bed, then the other. She put on her slippers and threw a coat over her pink nightgown.

"All right. I'll come."

She shuffled down the stairs, still only half awake. In the doctor's bedroom, she said:

"It's too hot in here. We must have a window open."

She went and opened it, then stood by the fireplace, waiting. Kuperus had closed the door, but, having done that, he didn't know what to say or what to do. He couldn't have said quite why he'd gone to get her.

"Did I hit you, too?" he asked without looking at her.

"It doesn't matter about me."

"And Beetje? Do you think she'll tell everybody?"

"Of course she will."

"What did she say?"

"She swore you must be crazy."

"Listen, Neel . . ."

"I'm listening."

"This is what we're going to do. . . . We'll pack our bags right away — tonight, in fact — and tomorrow we'll take the first train to Paris. . . ."

185

"You can take it if you like."

"Why not you?"

"Because I don't want to go."

"You mean you refuse to live with me? Answer me. Do you refuse?"

"I refuse to leave Holland."

"What's wrong with living in the South of France? In Nice, for instance... You'd have nothing to do the whole day long."

"I don't mind work."

He had never seen her calmer, more sure of herself. She rejected his offer with complete indifference. Going over to the window, she shut it a little, because a draft of cold air was moving across the room.

"I'm quite ready to help you pack."

"Look here, Neel! I mean this seriously. If you come with me, I'll marry you."

And still in the same offhand way, she answered:

"I won't go."

"Do you refuse to become my wife?"

"Yes."

"Why?"

"For no particular reason. Just because I don't want to."

"And if I stay here?"

"I'll go on keeping house for you. Now that I'm about it..."

Avoiding her eye, he paced up and down the room.

"Go to bed," he ordered.

"Here?"

"Yes, here."

He watched her in the mirror, saw her throw off her coat and slip into the bed.

"What about you? Aren't you coming to bed?"

"Not yet."

"You ought to take a sleeping pill."

No. He wasn't going to take a sleeping pill. He didn't want to sleep. He wanted to think. And think he did, furiously, angrily, reviewing one by one the events of the day, beginning with Groven's frigid politeness and De Greef's unconcealed contempt, right down to the ugly scene with Beetje, and ending with Neel's refusal to marry him.

"All right! Then I won't go either!" he suddenly announced emphatically.

He was expecting Neel to start arguing about it, or at least to show surprise, but when he turned toward the bed he found her more than half asleep, hardly able to keep her eyes open.

"Do you hear that, Neel? I won't go! I'm not afraid of them. . . . What can they do to me?"

"Why don't you come to bed?"

"You'll see if I don't know how to hit back! And no later than tomorrow either! They're all in league to hound me out of town. . . ."

She shut her eyes, and suddenly, looking at her, he remembered their first night, and felt the blood rush to his head.

"Do you hear what I say, Neel?"

And still the constant patter of the rain, apart from which all was silence. A dead world with just one little corner that was alive, this warm bed, warmed by Neel's sleeping body.

For she had fallen asleep, and merely gave a little grunt as he got into the bed beside her.

So much the worse for them, all of them! If they didn't like it, they'd just have to lump it! In a firm hand he had written:

Dear friend,
  Would you please come here as soon as you possibly can. I want to see you about a matter of the utmost importance.
  I am counting on you.
                                    Hans Kuperus

It was Neel who had taken it to Van Malderen's office. When she returned, Kuperus pounced on her in the hall.

"What did he say?"

"He asked if you were going away."

"What did you tell him?"

"That I didn't know."

"Is he coming?"

"He didn't say."

On the way back, she had bought some cutlets and lettuce. She went into the kitchen, and a moment later he could hear her making up the fire.

As for Kuperus, he went down to the cellar to get a bottle of Burgundy, which he put in its traditional place by the side of the stove. Then he got the tray ready with the wine glasses and some biscuits.

Mia was practicing again, but the sound no longer annoyed him. On the contrary, he now regarded it as a suitable accompaniment to the drama, serving to heighten his emotions.

He wasn't going! That was definitely decided. And not only was he staying, but he was going to take the offensive. He was going to do something altogether unexpected, which would completely turn the tables.

He saw Van Malderen's head pass the window, and shouted to Neel to open the door at the same moment the doorbell rang. But he remained in the dining room while Neel relieved the visitor of his coat.

"I've come, as you asked me. . . . What is it you want of me?"

He'd come straight to the point without a

word of friendly greeting. That was significant.

"I need your help. Sit down."

And the doctor poured two glasses of wine.

"Not for me, thanks," said Van Malderen. "Not at this time of day."

"Just as you like. . . . In any case, it's as a lawyer that I need your services. . . . I want to bring a suit."

He expected Franz to look surprised, if not to jump from his chair, but the lawyer merely frowned.

"I've been accused of murder. Various people have made it quite obvious by their attitude. And to vindicate my honor, I have only one recourse – to sue for defamation of character. . . ."

"Who?"

"I'm not quite sure. You'll have to advise me about that. But, for one, Groven. He summoned me to his office and then insulted me, grossly insulted me, in the presence of his clerk. . . ."

Van Malderen shrugged his shoulders.

"And there are others. For instance, my colleague De Greef, who only yesterday . . ."

"Excuse me," sighed Van Malderen, "but there's not the slightest use going on, because I can't act for you."

"You mean you refuse?"

"Definitely."

"As a lawyer, you refuse to act for a man who's being persecuted?"

"Both as a lawyer and as one of your oldest friends. Still more, as a sane man! The idea is absurd from start to finish. First, you wouldn't have a leg to stand on. Second, the case would be ridiculous and thoroughly unpleasant. Third. . . ."

"Yes? Third?"

"There are some causes that I would rather not defend. I have every right to pick and choose. If you want to waste your time, you can ask every lawyer in the country. You won't find one to take on a case like this."

He moved toward the door.

"Franz!" cried Kuperus.

"Well?"

"Is that your last word?"

"The last, yes, on this or any other subject!"

And without waiting for Neel to open the door, he took down his coat and walked out of the house.

The piano was still playing, and Kuperus stood with his elbows on the mantelpiece, staring at himself in the mirror. His features were puffy, his eyes tired, his mouth cruel. Permeating his whole being was a feeling of lassitude and at the same time a warm, tender self-pity.

They were all against him, the whole town.

191

They wanted at all costs to drive him out. But that only made him cling more tightly than ever to his little corner of the universe, his street, his house and all the things in it, and even the music that came through the wall.

He turned and looked at Alice's photograph, the one she'd had taken in Paris. For two or three minutes he gazed at it, and if there was pity in his eye, it was because in a strange way he included her in his pity for himself.

"I've got a cutlet for you," announced Neel, coming in to set the table.

He turned around. She looked tired, too. There was a droop in her shoulders and an irritable look on her face.

"What did he say?" she ventured to ask.

He shrugged his shoulders and answered, with a sigh:

"They're all against me."

"You see!"

"See what?"

"That you'd much better go."

She brought in his cutlet and after a moment's hesitation began:

"I've been thinking things over....I don't want you to do anything foolish. So, if you're really set on it, I'll come with you as far as Brussels. They say you can get along in Belgium speaking Dutch....I'd stay there a few weeks with you – long enough for you to get settled. Then I'd come back...."

It wasn't affection. It might have been pity. She made the proposal with an air of resignation.

"We could catch the early train tomorrow morning. We don't need long to pack."

"That's all over now. I'm not going."

"You're making a mistake."

"Why?"

"Because they'll force you to."

He flared up again:

"Nobody can force me to go. Do you hear that? They haven't got a particle of proof. Even if you went and told them about the letter, they still wouldn't have any proof. Nobody saw me do it, and they haven't found a thing that would enable them to fasten it on me...."

He went over to the window and looked out. The canal, the quay, with two trees that were not yet in leaf, the houses on the other side. A man passed, wheeling a barrow. Somewhere, bells were ringing. It was still raining.

His breath made the windowpane misty. Hanging on either side were curtains with crochetwork. It was Alice who had made those curtains. On the window sill was a beaten brass cachepot, which they'd bought in Brussels, where they'd been for their honeymoon.

Neel had gone back to the kitchen, leaving his cutlet on the table. Now that Beetje had left them, she preferred to eat in the kitchen, so that she could keep an eye on the stove.

Kuperus turned back into the room, but, instead of sitting down to his meal, he wandered into the living room. Everything was in its place, the piano, the music stool, Mia's plush cushion, the new furniture, and even the ball of sky-blue wool.

It was such a celestial blue, so utterly unreal, that he was touched. And when he picked it up, the feel of it was as delicate as the color.

Such purity, such grace!

On one of the needles was the little square of knitting already done. It was to have been a sweater. For indoors, Jane had said. . . .

He dropped it, picked it up, then put it firmly down, making a resolution never to look at it again. He wouldn't look at the photograph either. He sat down in one of the easy chairs, only to think that that was where he'd sat in the evening for fifteen years reading the *Telegraaf*, while the pink-shaded lamp threw its circle of soft light.

And they wanted to chase him away. What would he do with himself in Brussels, or Paris, or even on the Riviera? He would be an outcast, a wanderer with no roots, like Karl Vorberg. . . . He wouldn't even have Neel to share his bed. . . . He'd be left with nothing.

"Neel!" he called.

He was solemn, but she could see at once that he was in a state of intense emotion. She saw him sit down in front of his cutlet, which had by now got cold.

"Come and have your meal in here, will you? . . . Do as I ask you, Neel. We're going to have our lunch quietly and calmly. . . . Don't look at me like that. Sit down . . ."

"I'll just take the saucepan off the fire. . . ."

She came back in a moment, carrying her plate.

"You see, don't you? . . . There's no reason why we shouldn't be very happy together. What can they do to us? . . . Nothing! They can yap to their hearts' content, but what do I care? . . . I have money. I don't need any patients."

"You're not eating."

"No hurry. I'll eat my cutlet in a minute. . . . You see, I'm quite calm. . . . It's you who are not eating. . . ."

"I'm not hungry."

"But you must eat your lunch . . . or I'll be cross with you. . . . You're not afraid of me, are you?"

"No."

"Then you won't leave me. Ever!...We'll live here together, the two of us....You'll be able to have a good time. But you must make me a promise, Neel. Swear you'll never leave me. Swear on your mother's head."

She looked away, embarrassed.

"Why won't you swear?...Don't you mean to stay with me?"

She began to be frightened. His voice had changed. Had he suddenly remembered the decision he'd once made to kill her if ever she left him? Whatever it was, he was looking at her with strange eyes, bereft of thought.

"You know very well I'll stay."

"Then swear."

He was absolutely set on it. At all costs, he must have her promise on oath.

"I swear...."

"On your mother's head."

A little shiver went down her spine.

"On...on my...mother's head!"

The doctor's face lit up with almost childish joy.

"You see!"

"See what?"

"That everything's coming out all right. I knew it would. We'll stay here together, us two in our own home. We'll have our meals together, we'll sleep together. And I want you to start drinking wine."

"I don't like it."

"That doesn't matter. You'll get to."

And he poured her a full glass, which she didn't dare refuse.

"We'll open a bottle every day.... And in the evenings you'll sit here with some sewing, while I read the paper."

"Yes," she said dejectedly.

She couldn't even swallow the mouthful she'd been chewing for ages.

He got up and fetched the ball of blue wool.

"You must finish this knitting.... Yes, you must. I want you to."

She couldn't find a word to say. She simply sat there petrified, while the fire roared in the stove.

"Do you understand, Neel?... There's only one thing: I don't suppose they'll allow Mia to come here.... But we'll hear her just the same. We can send her some chocolates.... I expect there are still some in the sideboard, some of those we used to buy for her.... Do you know where Madame used to buy them?"

She nodded, speechless.

"Neel!"

He avoided catching sight of himself in the mirror, came back to his seat, and poured himself a glass of wine.

"Get me a cigar."

She had to pass behind him to get one of the boxes on the mantelpiece. When she turned around again, it was to see a rounded back and Kuperus's head buried in his arms on the table.

His shoulders heaved convulsively, while from his throat came raucous sobs that sounded as though they must be tearing him to bits.

"Doctor!" cried Neel, rushing toward him. "Calm yourself, Doctor!"

She couldn't think of anything else to say. She felt she must do something, but there was no stopping him now.

"Doctor!...Please!..."

She hovered around him, not knowing what to do. His suffering frightened her; it seemed so complete, so abysmal, as though it could never end.

"Doctor!...Please!..."

She wept, too, though for no reason. She had never seen a man cry before, and it filled her with shame.

She stood beside him, wondering whether she hadn't better leave him to himself, when he took one of his hands from under his head and, still sobbing, groped for her hand and squeezed it.

She heard the letter slot rattle and even the sound of a letter falling on the floor.

It was only a little boy, who, on a postcard, had scribbled the word *Murderer*.

Still hiding his face, Kuperus felt for his handkerchief.

NINE

"Look out! Here's the murderer!"

And at once the little boys would scatter, leaving the sidewalk free for Dr. Kuperus. Every day he went for a walk, and every day followed exactly the same route.

By the front door of his house there was still the brass plate that said:

DR. HANS KUPERUS
OFFICE HOURS 7 TO 11 A.M.

But nowadays nobody ever came. So to pass the time, he walked the streets with his hands in his pockets. And little by little his itinerary had been narrowed down until it was so invariable that anybody seeing him was apt to say:

"It must be ten o'clock. The doctor's just passed."

First of all he went along the unused canal, crossed the third bridge, and reached the main canal, where barges came from all directions loaded with produce.

A little farther on he came to the Van Malderens', and he never failed to look up at the veranda, where he'd be sure to see Jane bending over her sewing.

At eleven, by the cathedral, it was unusual if he didn't find a wedding or a funeral in progress. At half past he would be watching the children streaming out of school.

He looked at everything and remembered everything. Without a second's hesitation he could have said which day such and such lamppost had been newly painted. He knew if the postmen or milkmen were late or early on their rounds, and on market days he counted the cows, and listened to the farmers haggling over their prices.

One day he was passing the Town Hall when a painter fell off a scaffolding, and he had been one of the many people who had immediately crowded around. Rather shyly he had wormed his way to the front, and bent over the injured man.

With a lump in his throat, he had felt the man's head and limbs to see if any bones were broken. At the same time, he'd heard them ring the bell of one of his colleagues.

The latter had arrived on the scene, and without so much as a word had brushed Kuperus aside.

He had got used to it by now. It no longer hurt. In July, when all the windows were open, he had heard Mia's voice saying:

"There goes Uncle Kuperus."

And he distinctly heard her father's answer:

"You're not to call him Uncle Kuperus any more. . . . He isn't your uncle."

Another walk in the afternoon, and so the hours slipped by. On the stroke of five he pushed open the door of the Onder den Linden. Nobody greeted him. He was no longer president of the club, and his name had been removed from the board. The players went on with their games, pretending not to see him.

Old Willem went to the bar, put a bottle of beer and a small glass of gin on his tray, and set them down in front of the doctor without a word or a look. Kuperus put the exact money on the table, and the waiter took it after he had gone.

That didn't matter, however. As in the old days, the doctor had his seat, always the same one, and there he sat among his former friends, listening to their conversation, till it was time for him to go.

What went on in his mind was his affair. No one could guess his thoughts, not even Neel, in spite of her being the one person who had seen him weep.

She had written a letter to Karl, who was still in Amsterdam.

I think he's going crazy. I'm sure, anyhow, he can't go on much longer like this. Last week he sent for a notary and made his will. Everything's to come to me. He says he's got thirty thousand guilders in the bank, and there's the house, which belongs to him too....

At seven o'clock every evening Kuperus inserted his key in the lock and sank back once again into the atmosphere of his house, an atmosphere as calm, as stagnant as the water in the old canal, an atmosphere in which the passage of a human being seemed to have no effect whatever. Doors creaked when opened, as though they had been shut for many months.

He hung up his hat and coat, and didn't forget to glance at himself in the mirror, apparently satisfied with his blank features, in which neither thought nor feeling could be read.

The table was set. Neel brought in the dinner and sat down opposite him.

"Van Malderen made a break of forty-two," he announced in exactly the same way as if he'd played with him himself. "He's taking his wife to Ostend for a few days' holiday."

She answered cautiously, well aware that a

203

single misplaced word would be enough to throw him into a rage. For what he wanted of her was something impossible, impossible even to explain.

When they were sitting like that in the evenings at the dinner table, Neel was to be Neel no longer. He had even made her alter Alice's dresses, so that she could wear them, and he had persuaded her little by little to change the way she did her hair.

And after the meal was cleared away, she had to come and sit with him in the circle of soft light and do her needlework.

She had already finished knitting the sky-blue sweater, and the day she had refused to wear it he had made the worst row they had ever had, shouting and storming till all the neighbors heard.

As usual, Kuperus, in his slippers, sat reading the paper with a cigar between his lips. From time to time, without looking up, he would read her a passage.

"A typhoon in the Philippines has caused the death of five hundred people."

Or:

"In a mining accident in the United States, thirty-eight miners have been buried alive."

She knew she must avoid the least thing that could set him off, but just what that might be was difficult to foresee. It varied with each day. Sometimes it was a word, sometimes a gesture, sometimes a silence.

Then suddenly the doctor's features would harden, and the paper would drop. His eyes would stare into space like those of a man who sees other things than those visible to the common run of mortals.

"Half a guilder!" he groaned.

There was no use her going away. That would only precipitate a crisis. There was no use her protesting. All she could do was to wait in silence, her eyes bent on her work.

Kuperus got up and came and stood in front of her. He began in a sarcastic tone, but the sarcasm soon turned to bitterness.

"Half a guilder!...Isn't that right, Neel?... It all happened for a mere half-guilder! If there'd not been a mistake of half a guilder in the change, my wife would never have said anything to you, you'd never have got your own back by writing me the letter...."

He walked up and down the room. He had said it all before, even in the same words, except that the words were harsher the more Burgundy he'd drunk.

"...in that case she'd be sitting here now in

your place, and you'd be in the kitchen. . . ."

His eyes became more and more inhuman. It was impossible to believe they saw the same things as other people. He looked at things as though they were transparent, or as though they were living beings.

Alice's photograph was still there, and no evening passed without his gazing at it.

"Do you understand now?. . .All that for a matter of fifty cents!. . .Because the housekeeping money was half a guilder out!"

He didn't need any answers to whet his anger. It rose by itself, goaded only by the memories with which his mind was burdened.

And it ended in the same way.

"Get out!. . .Go to bed!. . .I can't stand the sight of you any longer!"

Silently, obediently, Neel got up and went. Reaching her attic, she left the door open, and she could still hear him striding up and down the room, talking to himself. She undressed and went to bed, but kept her coat handy, because she knew the sequel.

An hour later Kuperus had gone to bed. But he hadn't tossed about for ten minutes before he got up and went to the door.

"Neel!" he called.

He couldn't sleep alone. When she joined him, he pretended to have forgotten his recent rage.

"Come to bed...Get me a glass of water will you? And my pills..."

He could no longer do without sleeping pills. For another quarter of an hour she heard him sigh and groan, while she mused, staring into the darkness.

She had to go farther afield for her shopping nowadays, because in the shops where she was known people began to be disagreeable. Rumor had coupled her with the doctor's guilt. Some even went so far as to say she'd been his mistress for years, and that the two had put their heads together to get rid of Mme Kuperus.

According to age and temperament, imagination did its work. For the children, Kuperus became a sort of supernatural monster, not far removed from Satan himself, and their blood ran cold in their veins if he came upon them unawares.

And what could little Mia think when she paused in her practicing and heard her ex-uncle Kuperus pacing up and down, up and down?

"Mind you don't ever speak to him!"

"What would he do to me?"

"He'd kill you!"

Kuperus knew all about that. He could feel it in the air. With his heavy regular stride he walked alone, and in the Onder den Linden he noticed that the billiard players — particularly the younger ones — often missed a shot just because he was staring at them.

They didn't know! No one knew what he was thinking, because he had escaped from their world and entered another, which existed for him alone.

As a small boy he had always, on waking, looked first at one of the flowers on the wallpaper, which looked — no doubt in his eyes only — like the head of Vercingetorix, as depicted in his history book. The interesting thing about it was the great variety of its expressions, sometimes smiling, sometimes scowling. It was only after a long time that he discovered what the variations depended on: the exact position from which he looked. After that he was able to make Vercingetorix smile or scowl just as he wished.

It was rather like that now. The town of Sneek, as other people knew it, no longer existed for him. He had re-created it according to his own whim, like the head of Vercingetorix, which, to his mother, was merely one of the flowers on the wallpaper.

Each building he passed on his daily walks had its own special significance for him. Like the house opposite the school. He had lived there when he was six years old. He'd had a bow and arrows then, and had drawn a target on one of the walls. When rubbing it out, someone had broken a piece of brick off the corner and the gap still showed.

A little farther on he jumped back fourteen years — since time no longer counted — to a certain day when he and Alice had paid a visit to some friends who had just had a baby, and they had gone home full of hope themselves. . . . Farther still . . .

But it wasn't necessary to go far; his own world followed him everywhere, his own special world, with its own particular mystery, which would never leave him in peace, and so often in the evening made him fly into a rage.

The mystery of Neel's half-guilder! If the change had been right that day, his whole life would have been different! He'd still have his waiting room crowded with patients, and go to see others in the afternoon. . . . He'd be waked up at night to go make deliveries. . . .

"What is it?" he'd ask out of the window, before deciding whether to go down.

And if it didn't sound urgent, he'd merely grunt:

"I'll come around tomorrow."

Or else:

"Put some compresses on, and wait till I see him."

Half a guilder! But there was more to it than that. Something more, which he knew, but nobody else did. Nobody. Neither Van Malderen, nor Anton Groven, nor Dr. De Greef, nor the people he passed in the street.

As he looked at them all, he couldn't keep a disdainful smile from coming to his lips. Because in them he recognized the man he had been before.

For instance, when Pijpekamp said to his friends in the café:

"I'm going to Paris tomorrow."

The doctor's eyes twinkled. Because Pijpekamp was going to Paris, they were all slightly uneasy, disgusted with their commonplace lives, their little town, their eternal billiards.

And when they saw a love story on the screen at the movie house across the way, they were tired of their wives and hankered after a heroine. . . .

They were all the same, the grocer, the butcher, the man with the bicycle shop, and every passerby — they all wanted what they didn't have; they all wanted to escape.

Just what he had wanted before! And to get what he had wanted, he had killed someone, killed two people!

It had started with half a guilder. . . . From that to a servant's revenge. . . And from that again to the longing of a middle-aged man to kick over the traces, to break out of the rut.

That was all! And nobody knew. He was the only one to have discovered that circle and to know why every day he passed the same place at exactly the same time.

Because he had escaped! Only to return as quickly as possible, terrified by the emptiness he had escaped into. He had returned, and now clung to every wall, to every house, to every memory, to every habit, to the box of cigars on the mantelpiece, the bottle of Burgundy warming up by the side of the fire, right down to the familiar clack of the billiard balls in the Onder den Linden.

Patiently he went on his little daily round, never tiring of it.

And at seven he got home, thrust his keys into the lock just as he had done for fifteen years, and in the hall he was greeted by the same smell of floor polish.

The table was set. Neel brought in the dinner.

He no longer desired her. He no longer touched her. If he kept her there, it was as a sort of hostage.

"I had a letter from Karl. He's lost some money at the races and says will you send him some more?"

Of course he would! What did that matter to him?

What he didn't know – and there were, after all, some things concealed from him – was what Neel had answered that afternoon at the kitchen table.

I threw the pack of powder down the toilet, because I was scared of it. It seemed to me they'd suspect the truth at once. In any case, I don't think this can go on much longer. Each day he gets a little queerer. Sometimes at night he makes me hold his hand while he goes to sleep.

Neel was wearing one of Alice's dresses. She'd had to shorten the waist. There were veal cutlets for dinner. Kuperus asked:

"Have you brought up a bottle of Burgundy?"

"Yes. There are only fifteen bottles left."

He drank freely; therefore, there'd be a scene that night, perhaps a violent one, with the whole story over again, right from the half-guilder to the end.

Meanwhile, there was time to eat in peace and even perhaps sew for a quarter of an hour. She also kept some sewing up in her room, so that she had something to do while she was waiting for him to call her down again.

"Jane Van Malderen has got the flu," he announced.

Van Malderen had said so an hour ago in the Onder den Linden.

He had to lead up to the row with little phrases like that, of no particular importance, interspersed by silences, by the rustling of the newspaper, and by the reading of little extracts from it, generally about accidents, which seemed to give Kuperus a peculiar satisfaction.

"The airplane that crashed into the North Sea yesterday is reported to have been carrying seven passengers. . . ."

Neel sighed and waited patiently. . . .

Combloux
December 1935

THORNDIKE PRESS HOPES you have enjoyed this Large Print book. All our Large Print titles are designed for the easiest reading, and all our books are made to last. Other Thorndike Press Large Print books are available at your library, through selected bookstores, or directly from the publisher. For more information about current and upcoming titles, please call us, toll free, at 1-800-223-6121, or mail your name and address to:

THORNDIKE PRESS
P. O. BOX 159
THORNDIKE, MAINE 04986

There is no obligation, of course.